Barry and Bev
The Big concert

Barry and Bev
The Big concert

Rita May

Matador
9 Priory Business Park,
Wistow Road, Kibworth Beauchamp,
Leicestershire. LE8 0RX
Tel: 0116 279 2299
Email: books@troubador.co.uk
Web: www.troubador.co.uk/matador
Twitter: @matadorbooks

ISBN 978 1785898 570

British Library Cataloguing in Publication Data.
A catalogue record for this book is available from the British Library.

Printed and bound in the UK by TJ International, Padstow, Cornwall
Typeset in 11pt Aldine401 BT by Troubador Publishing Ltd, Leicester, UK

Matador is an imprint of Troubador Publishing Ltd

My Mother
Elsie Gilbert
25.10.1922 – 08.07.2015

BEV

It's my birthday today, forty-three. Wonder what the next year will hold for me? I certainly hope it's going to be better than the last.

I've been thinking about life and death a lot of late. I mean, we are so very quickly forgotten. I hardly ever give Barbara next door a thought and she's only been dead about three months; she never enters my head, even when I'm wearing her shoes.

Now all this thinking I've been doing has led me to make a very important decision. Actually I got the idea from an American magazine. The Americans are a bit different, shall we say. So, I've decided I'm going to order my coffin on my sixtieth birthday.

That will certainly shock Barry. I can't wait to see his poor face when they deliver it to the house. If we are still together, that is, and it's getting more and more likely that we won't be.

"Sign here, sir, one empty coffin, teak with brass handles."

I'm going to put it in the back bedroom, then I can start my work on it.

I want something different, something that shouts out loud about me and what I am and represent. Something that will make people remember me.

My plans are to paint it a bright yellow – yellow is a

happy colour, the colour of sunshine. Then I am going to stick transfers all down the sides. Like the ones they put on the sides of small cars – butterflies, flowers, a wreath that looks like a Walnut Whip. Oh – and most importantly, a little message down the side in big letters for all the mourners to see.

FIRE RESISTANT.

Lots of mystified voices, following me down the aisle.

"Oh my god! It's *fire resistant!*"

"Bloody hell! It must be made of some sort of metal."

"*Metal!* No chance of that burning then, even at them temperatures."

"Poor Bev, it'll slow-cook her."

The speculation will go on and on; they'll be phoning the crematorium to make sure I've gone up. Or down, in my case.

I want my descendants to remember me, and what better way than having a tale like that to tell and pass down the generations? I want to become a legend. I've certainly no intention of being forgotten in a hurry.

I was more than a bit tiddly when I went to work this afternoon. Afternoons, grrrrr, I hate bloody afternoons, and tough luck: I'm on them permanent. Last in gets the crap shifts. I suppose I could have rung in with dizzy spells, which I did have, after all the booze. But I did that last week, the boss knows it's my birthday and she's smart enough to put two and two together and get the right answer. I hope she didn't notice my staggered walk and slurred speech. I tried to keep away from her as much as

I could without raising suspicion. But she is not daft – far from it.

The reason for my drunken stupor was that my three very best friends, Cheryl, Rose and Geraldine, took me out for a birthday brunch. I've never had bacon, eggs, sausage, mushrooms, beans, tomatoes, black pudding, not forgetting the fried bread, three glasses of lager, one whisky and pep and two glasses of red wine, plus one full packet of Polo mints all in one lunchtime. No wonder my stomach was a bit off. But I must say, a fabulous time was had by all.

Bless them, they've clubbed together and bought me a portable 'non-invasive liposuction therapy machine'. You stick it on your fat bits for an hour and it freezes the fat cells to death, then they pass through your body and out. Quite ingenious if it works, fingers crossed, we will see.

Rose was very excited; she's joined one of the online dating sites, and she said at £12.99 a month she hopes she gets at least one bonk out of it. I know she couldn't stand him but I think she's still missing that cheating ex-husband of hers.

Geraldine has promised me her mother Sandra's Stetson for the line dancing at the club. It's practically new. Well, Sandra doesn't need it anymore, she's gone to that place in the sky, bless her. Geraldine's going to drop it in at work for me.

Didn't get a card from Barry this morning; I saw him look at my cards and then he went out. When I got in from my afternoon shift there was a card and a box of chocolates. I just left them where he'd placed them. I did keep looking at the chocolates though, but I managed to resist. I have got my pride.

BARRY

I committed the cardinal sin. I forgot Bev's birthday. Her fault really – if we'd been talking she would have been hinting for the last week or so. Women are the obsessive birthday people. It's always been their place to remind us men, we rely on it. So it's their fault really – if they don't remind us they can't shout about not getting one.

Saw the bank manager again about the club's finances. They're in a pretty bad state. He said if we don't do something quick we're heading for closure. I thought, *I bloody know that, mate.*

As the secretary of the club, I feel I should be able to come up with some great scheme that'll get us out of the shit. But I'm at a loss to know what to do. I've called a committee meeting for tomorrow night; see what we can come up with. This village would be dead without the club.

I've just heard that the Carlton Miners' Welfare has gone into liquidation. Bloody shame, it was a good club. They're dropping like flies. Aldi have bought it, another supermarket, as though there aren't enough already.

The youngsters are just not frequenting the clubs nowadays. I reckon that eventually they'll all disappear. The end of an era.

I didn't get the trolley man job at Sainsbury's. They've filled all the vacancies; I didn't even get an interview. They obviously don't think I'm good enough to round up a few shopping trollies and put them under a shelter. Or is it that at forty-five I am just too old? Bloody marvellous – I'm a construction engineer. Five years at college, then twenty-odd years at Shaw Brothers until they folded. Head of department for eleven years.

What's it coming to, eh? They reckon we're all going to have to work till we're seventy. Where, at what? Bring it on, I say, bring it on.

Decided to go for a walk down the woods this afters; it cheers me up down there. Saw a lovely little grey squirrel – couldn't have been very old. He just stared at me. I tried to stare him out, but it was me that moved first. Cheeky little beggar, he was, or she, as it may be. I suppose they think we are encroaching on their territory, which we humans are, all the time. I've never thought about it before but squirrels can walk down trees as well as up. It's amazing really. Man has got the greatest brain in all of the animal kingdom but some of the things the other species can do, it's just mind-boggling. I am feeling like shit.

BEV

Love my new Stetson. Wonder if it will affect Geraldine when we're line dancing, though. Her glancing at her mother's Stetson on my head, thinking for a second it's her mother, then seeing my face under it. It was ever such a sad to do. Her mother was fine when we were dancing to *One Step Forward (Two Steps Back)*. We always finish on that; it's one of my favourites. Next thing, she's dead at the chip van. She'd just asked for some scraps on her chips, when she keeled over and fell face down. She'd taken her hat off, thank goodness, or it would have been covered in mud like her face, poor woman.

The Stetson is a light brown with darker brown tassels hanging from the back. It's really nice to say it was Sandra's; she'd never been known to have great fashion sense. I've got a couple of American-style badges I can pin on it. Mine is getting a bit raggy so I'm happy to have it.

The chip van's been moved into the club car park now. It was crazy having it on the grass verge; all your shoes got muddy. Now if anybody keels over with a heart attack, they'll bash their face on the tarmac. Oh well, you can't have it all!

I lay on the bed and tried out my non-invasive liposuction thingy. You have to keep it on for an hour so I did a bit of reading on my Kindle. After the hour session my belly was like a piece of ice. So I filled a hot water bottle and put it on my belly. Now the question is, will the heat of the water bottle negate the cold of the liposuction thingy and warm the fat cells back up again, so they don't die and get flushed away? I just don't know. The instruction booklet is in Chinese.

Took old Connie next door a piece of my birthday cake, she was ever so grateful, bless her.

BARRY

Committee meeting went well. The lads came up with some ideas. One that we are definitely going to put into action is a Saturday night big concert. Get a top-class act, advertise in the local papers and shops and see if we can bring some extra punters in. It's a risk, it might fall flat, but we have to try.

We had a visit from the police today at the club. They said they were called out in the early hours of Sunday morning, as all the security lights were on. Turns out it was our concert secretary, Sam, bonking Big Rita round the back of the club. I told him, "Having the lights blazing costs the club money."

Baz said, "What does he want to bonk her in the light for? She's got a face like the back end of a tram smash." They are a refined lot.

BEV

Exciting news: Barry is organising a big concert at the club. I must get myself something new to wear. I've seen a lovely royal blue top with a big sequinned butterfly on the front. Got an excuse to go and buy it now.

There's a letter for Barry; it says on the envelope, *Marks and Spencer*. I keep looking at it – I'd love to open it, but he'd go mad if I did. I know he's applied for a job at Marks'. Please let him get a job. Marks' would be great. I heard they do a right good staff discount. It's getting him down and it's getting me down. He needs a job. I need him to get a job. He's only forty-five, for Christ's sake. He's got another twenty years or more of working life. He can't be out of work all that time. I hope not, anyway. I'd cut my wrists.

Geraldine rang; she said everybody is excited about the big concert. It's the talk of the village. She's got a new red off-the-shoulder top and slinky black trousers. Lucky beggar, she has the figure to carry it off. I'd look like Giant Haystacks in drag. Can't stand showing off my arms.

It is time we had some decent acts at the club. Last Saturday they had this soprano, she must have been seventy if she was a day. She sang *Love is Like a Violin* and asked us all to join in. Us lasses looked at each other: *gone out*. I mean, who knows the words to *Love is Like a Violin*? Silly cow.

BARRY

Brilliant, I've actually got an interview with Marks and Spencer's.

First interview I've had in four months. Yes, I think I'd make a bloody good security man. I'm the right build anyway. Saw one in Marks' the other day. He was stood looking spaced out, biting his fingernails. I know it could have been worse; he could have been picking his nose or scratching his arse.

I thought, *Blimey, I could do better than that.*

Better get my hair cut. I must take my grey suit to the cleaners and buy a blue shirt. Blue is Marks and Spencer's uniform colour. Make the interviewer feel like they're already talking to one of their own, and who knows, fingers crossed. I'd cross my bloody balls if I thought it would work. I know life at home would be less fraught if I could get a job. Bev goes on and on at me.

Called in at Connie's next door, she wanted some bits from Sainsbury's. She's always got a cuppa and a biscuit ready for me when I get back. Bless her, she's a good neighbour. I think me and Bev are probably the only people she sees. Makes you think there's nothing to get old for.

IMPORTANT NOTE: must make sure we order enough beer for the big concert. It's a gamble; I hope it pays off. They reckon this comedian I've booked has a big following. Fingers crossed they follow him to the Kenthorpe Miners' Welfare.

BEV

I'm feeling right down of late. We've had another bust-up. Two cups broken. It's amazing how little things can blow up. I was only telling him what to say at his interview with Marks and Spencer's. But he won't be told. He's always the same, a blooming know-all. It's getting that we hardly give each other a civil word these days.

I feel it's all too much for a body. I'm going to lie on the bed and place my non-invasive liposuction thingy on my belly. Have the hot water bottle at the ready and watch the gorgeous Gerard Butler in *Phantom of the Opera*; that always bucks me up. Gerard Butler – is he not just the sexiest man in the world? Oh, and I've got a bottle of wine and a Mars bar.

BARRY

The beer has been delivered to the club. We're borrowing a hundred chairs from the community centre. We've stocked the bar up with spirits and all the other stuff folk drink these days. Made sure we have enough bingo cards and pens; it's amazing how many people come to play bingo and don't bring a pen.

We've bought five hundred cheap pint glasses from Macro. Yes, I think we are ready for the big concert. I must check the toilet roll stocks. There's so much to think about. It's so important this concert goes well. The club is on its knees financially. Clubs are closing down around us, right, left and centre. It's bloody time-consuming, this secretary's job. Sometimes I wish I'd never taken it on.

BEV

Went to visit Rose for a cuppa and a chat. Nothing new on the dating front, she says. She doesn't have much luck with fellas, poor lass. She's been on her own about two years now. Her husband, Mike, just up and took off with their neighbour.

Rose came home from work one day and they'd both gone, vanished. They must have been in a hurry, she said, because they'd backed right over her lupins. I must say she seemed more upset about the lupins than him. I never liked him.

But the events that preceded that episode were unbelievable. It was the news event of the decade around these parts. Folk were talking about it for months. Rose nearly went into hiding.

Her neighbour's partner had got killed eight months previous. It was on both the BBC and ITV national news; place was full of reporters. They were a pair of show-offs, the neighbours – you know the type. Two lions stuck on top of the gateposts. Looked ridiculous, they did, way out of place on a council estate. Kids used to throw eggs at them; they were a blooming eyesore. Standard rose trees with roses on them in the front garden. Posh, bright yellow open-topped car with transfers of lions on the sides. They were obsessed with lions.

Well, on this particular day (so the story goes), their posh open-topped car smashed, full-on, bang into one of them big cranes that mend bridges and stuff. They reckon the car was doing about 170 miles an hour along the bypass.

Apparently, when the emergency services arrived to cordon it off and untangle the car from the crane they realised the driver had done a bunk. Then they noticed this person in the bushes watching them. The police kept shouting, asking if it was the missing driver. When they went to investigate, they found the missing driver alright, but only the head: there was not a body in sight. A decapitated head, eyes wide open, staring at them.

Freaked everybody out, it did. One of the coppers, they reckoned he must have been about six foot ten and eighteen stone, fainted. The paramedics had to place his head between his legs.

Then after a frantic search they found the body wedged

upside down in the branches of a conker tree – good job she was wearing trousers. (So much for driving in an open-top car.)

We heard it was a right to-do. I was at work, otherwise I would have gone and had a look.

Some of the coppers were having counselling for months. Folks said that when they went to see her in the chapel of rest you could see the join where the pathologist had sewn her head back on to her body. Big stitches right across her throat. Michelle Brown said they'd sewn it on lopsided. It veered to the left, she said, and she should know: she is a nurse. Folk were going in their droves.

Other than her husband occasionally dressing up in women's clothes, Rose said she had absolutely no idea he was gay.

I love Rose to bits, she's one of my best mates; she's a lovely person. I hope she doesn't come a cropper with this dating thingy. I know she's lonely, I really hope it works for her.

My boss, Barbara, has recommended some slimming tablets. I'm going to try them.

BARRY

It's been a great – no, double great – night at the club. Best Saturday night we've had for years. It was chock-a-block. I haven't seen it that full for yonks. Bar takings must have been well up.

Dennis came into the office, a big grin on his face – he's an ugly bastard. Should get them bloody teeth fixed.

"Great, int it?" he said. "I've just had to queue for a piss."

"It means they're drinking, putting money over the bar," I said, "and if it means queuing for a piss, so be it."

"Oh, I am happy for it," he said.

"We should have thought to put the beer up a couple of coppers."

Baz said, "We'll remember that if we have another."

Charlie 'Chuff' Leeds, top comedian, he did two forty-five-minute spots and had them howling, dead funny. Bit mucky, mind, and a bit pricey. I am just hoping it was worth it. We will see when the takings are added up.

Sam the Man was strutting around the club, taking all the credit as the concert secretary. He hasn't done a bloody thing, I've done it all. He didn't even book the act and that's his job. He's an idle git.

I saw Mable and Gladys pull a face at the comedian. They said he wasn't funny. I don't think they understood his smut. I'm going to have to tell them again about blocking the entrance with their scooters. Dennis went his full length over one of them last week, dropped all his fish and chips. Before he could get to his feet, a blooming big Doberman Pinscher slavered all over his chips and ran off with his haddock. He was fuming. He had six bags of crisps instead.

The punters came from all over to see this Charlie Chuff bloke. The car park was chock-a-block. Baz got his car bumped, not badly, but it set him off on one. They'd buggered off, so we don't know who did it. He said if he found out who'd pranged it, he'd prang them. And he would.

Aye, I reckon it was a success tonight; I bet the bar takings are well up. On the other hand, one successful night isn't going to get the bank manager off our backs.

I didn't see our lass in the club tonight. It was busy though, and I was busy in the office. She was in bed when I got in, so I didn't disturb her; she's been working today so she'll be tired.

BEV

It is the early hours of the morning. I have been to bed but I couldn't sleep. I heard Barry the Bastard come in. he's snoring away now.

I am in a bloody foul mood. I am sat at the kitchen table with a bottle of Shiraz, gorging on the gingerbread men that I've bought for the grandkids when they come for their tea tomorrow. Bang goes the diet again. I'm not bothered; I'll stay a fat slob. There's loads of women a lot fatter than me. I'll throw the bloody slimming tablets in the bin, and the non-invasive liposuction thingy can go to the charity shop.

I work my guts out at that flaming petrol station. I wish it was flaming. I often feel like putting a match to it. I wonder if I am a frustrated pyrotechnician? Good job I don't smoke because when I'm feeling that way I might just do it. Be a right blaze, it would.

I work all the unsocial hours that them with kids won't do.

I was really looking forward to the big concert at the club with me mates. They reckon the comedian was absolutely brilliant.

I rushed home from work – I don't get in till ten past eight – got ready, put mi new butterfly sequinned top on. My hair went right for a change. I felt really good and I thought I looked good as well.

Then when I got to the club, the concert room was full. Slimy Sam wouldn't let us in, and I'm the secretary's wife, for Christ's sake.

"Fire regulations," he said. He's a bossy, officious git. No wonder his wife ran off with the egg man. They reckon the concert room had been full from half past six.

Anyway, me and the lasses – there was Rose, Cheryl, Geraldine and a few others; the usual suspects – stood in the lobby with our drinks. We were pissed off. Then Cheryl popped her head into the Men Only room.

She said, "There're some empty seats in there."

We looked at each other for a second, wondering if we dare, and then all together we said, "Aye, why not?"

Well, you should have heard the rumpus from the oldies. There was about a dozen of us women invaded their little den.

Albert stood up and shouted, "Club rule number fifty-seven. Any woman that enters or tries to enter the Men Only room will be barred from the club." He's a daft bat.

Then old Charlie, who limps about with his stick, looking for sympathy, was off like a shot. He'd have done well in the hundred metres. The looks and comments we

15

got when we settled into a game of dominoes you wouldn't believe.

Then Slimy Sam, that bloody big-headed committee man, came rushing in, breathing heavy as though he'd just run the marathon, his veins sticking out all red on his neck. Charlie followed him, wiping the sweat from his forehead. Nearly physically pulled us off our chairs, they did, you'd have thought we were under arrest for committing armed robbery. It was no good arguing, we'd have been at it all night.

So we told them where to stick their exclusive Men Only room. Up their doodahs. Had to laugh as we were leaving.

Rose shouts, "It stinks of farts in here anyway. It must be the farting capital of the world." We were helpless; don't know why because it wasn't that funny. I think you had to be there.

So we all of us went into The Bell, and got ourselves halfway to being sozzled. Clive, the landlord, was very pleased. We had a good laugh though, calling the men some horrible, nasty names.

God, it's three o'clock. I'll just finish this bottle of Shiraz.

I could kill Barry, I could. I ought to poison him – I wonder where you can buy cyanide? I've never seen it in Sainsbury's.

Knife him? No, too messy.

Shoot him? No, haven't got a gun.

That's it then, I'll have to let him live.

I could smother him? Yes, that's it. I'll smother him with my orthopaedic pillow.

I feel blooming lousy. I'm pissed.

BARRY

Bev wasn't up when I left for the committee meeting this morning. So I didn't know she was still mad at me, till I got home for me roast beef and Yorkshires and there weren't any. I asked where the dinner was. She said she would sooner burn all her shoes than cook me a dinner. I should have known. She was in a foul mood last night. Out of her head, she was.

She came into my bedroom in the middle of the night and I thought she was going to get in bed with me – she was carrying her pillow, and she won't sleep anywhere without that orthopaedic pillow. I thought, *Oh God, no, I hope she's not expecting sex*. But then as she was staggering towards me, she stubbed her big toe on the foot of the bed. Ow – I felt it for her.

She let out this deafening howl, hopped about a bit on one leg, fell backwards into the wardrobe and sat in the bottom, staring at me for a bit, her eyes all crossed. It couldn't have been very comfy because she was sat on all me shoes. I suppose there are some times when it's handy to have a bit of fat around your posterior. I thought for a minute she'd gone to sleep. Then she hiccupped; I think that must have woke her because she scrambled out on all fours, tried to get up a few times, but couldn't.

So she pulled herself up by the dressing table. I never realised before how solid this bedroom furniture is. Then – I couldn't believe it – she started to rant and rave at me, saying it was my fault. I'd never shifted from me bloody bed.

It must be the menopause. I sometimes wish I'd lived in the Middle Ages. Men wouldn't have had to put up with wives in the menopause because the average life expectancy was only about thirty.

I tried to get her back to her own bed, but she wouldn't let me.

She slept half the night on the floor, her body sprawled on the landing with her head dangling over the top stair. She was too drunk to shift and I didn't want to do my back in; she is certainly no lightweight. I put a towel under her face because she was dribbling on to the stair carpet. She was shouting about being pushed out of the Men Only room. I hadn't got a clue what she was on about. It wasn't long before she was snoring away.

Bev is drinking too much, for sure. It took me ages then to drop off.

Anyway, it turns out the bar takings were up by 309% last night. So this dinnertime the committee put it to the vote and we've decided to have a big concert every Saturday night.

Our Julie came over with the kids. I took them to the park, had a game of footy. He's a little mardy-arse sometimes, our Morten – because he didn't get a goal, he deliberately kicked the ball in the pond.

I tried to reach it, nearly fell full-length in the water. Got all the bottoms of me trousers wet. They thought it was hilarious, the kids. I told him I'm not buying another ball. Took the kids back and then went to the chippy. I was starving.

Rose served me and gave me a mouth full of abuse. It appears the women couldn't get seats in the concert room so they ended up in The Bell. That's why Bev has been looking at me like she wants to slit my throat. I didn't know they couldn't get a seat. It was busy on Saturday night. I only left the office for a pee, and you had to queue right down past the slot machine.

I asked Rose for fish, chips and mushy peas. I saw her eyes scan the fish, then she served me the smallest; there weren't many chips either. You're at the mercy of the server in the chip shop if they've got narks on with you. It means settling with what they give you, or having a confrontation. I was that hungry I decide to have the confrontation, so I asked for a bigger fish, and she said they were all ordered. What a load of bollocks. Then I asked for more chips. She gave me a dirty look and shovelled about another three on to my tray. They are vindictive, some folk.

I bet the women will go ballistic when they find out that the committee have voted to have big concerts every Saturday. Ah well, we'll take care of that when it happens.

BEV

I've been in a right state all weekend. I could have done without our Julie and the kids coming on Sunday afternoon.

When they visit, she just leaves the kids to me and her dad. She just sits reading or watching the telly, oblivious to the fact that I work all week.

All of my body's hurting. I've got a stiff neck and my right big toe feels like an elephant's stamped on it, doesn't half hurt. I don't know what I've done to it. It's all bruised and red with a bit of blue. I hope it doesn't go septic. I go septic ever so easily, me. I've got this lousy headache that I can't shift. My body feels like I've done five rounds with Mike Tyson.

I got rat-arsed Saturday night. I know I like a drink but I went too far. Never again, not worth it!

God, would I love to win the lottery. For a start I would go on a long holiday, then I would tell the boss where to shove the bloody job – up her posterior.

Mable and Gladys won the jackpot in the club tonight, £195. Barry's face dropped to his boots; he was hoping it wouldn't be won for a few more weeks so they could accumulate more funds.

They are lucky, them two, they're always wining the bingo. If they fell off the top of Blackpool Tower they'd fall on top of somebody carrying a mattress.

Last time I won anything it was in Skegness, a lamp. I got a right shock when I plugged it in: it worked. Ha ha.

Got me new uniform at work today; been without one for two months. My old one was a size twenty-four but I couldn't fasten the buttons so I asked for a size twenty-six. The dozy devils sent a size twenty-eight. Mind you, it's a good job they did; I can only just fasten it. Must be really small sizing – the company will have paid practically nothing for them, so you can't expect the sizes to be correct.

Oh admit it, woman, you're fat. I look in the mirror and I see this blooming whale. I've got to do something about it. Easiest solution: get rid of all the mirrors. Ha ha. Good job I've got a sense of humour or I'd slit my throat.

BARRY

I've got my interview with Marks and Spencer's coming up. I hope that goes well. I must pick up my suit from the cleaners.

The committee have decided to raise the membership fee from £5 to £10, and associate members – the women, that is – from £3 to £5. It'll bring a little bit of extra cash in, and anything is better than nothing.

Looked up Marks and Spencer's on the internet; it was founded in 1884 in Leeds, so it's a good old Yorkshire company. They have 703 stores and 81,223 employees. I really hope I'm going to be the 81,224th.

I'll remember all that and try and slip it into the interview, see if I can impress them.

BEV

I can't believe it. I got in from work and there's a message on the answerphone for Barry from Slimy Sam, or Mr Concert Secretary, as he likes to be addressed. He said he's spoken to the variety agent and he's sending some great top acts to the club starting this Saturday. Barry's never mentioned it. Well he wouldn't, would he? So what is going to happen now then? They don't allow seat-saving, and most of us women have commitments. I don't finish my afternoon shift till eight. They'll just have to allow us in the Men Only, it's as simple as that. Bugger rule fifty-seven.

Put me new uniform in the washer, and must have left a pair of his red underpants in there, silly sod that I am. My uniform is now pink and navy instead of white and navy. Don't know what the boss at work is going to say.

Connie was at her door as I was leaving for work, and she was upset. Her sister had died. I calmed her down and said I would pop in after work. Which I did, I stayed a good hour. I said me or Barry would take her to the funeral.

Craziest funeral I've ever been to was Geraldine's mother's. Baz and Geraldine's three brothers had been cajoled by Geraldine into carrying Sandra's coffin from the hearse into the church. Well, you might know Baz, as per usual, had been at the club boozing.

He was at the front, and as he stepped up to the pedestal where they place the coffin, he didn't lift his foot high enough, so he stumbled. The coffin went right down at his corner and hit the pedestal with a thump. Then we heard a scream echoing around the church – well, it sounded as if it came from inside the coffin. It shocked everybody for a moment. Eyes were popping out all over.

Then Christine Gordon put her hands in the air and shouted, "It's okay, it's okay, it was me that screamed, not the cadaver. I'm sure she'll be dead. They give them a brain test these days to make sure. Sorry."

Then she gave a nervous half-smile, turned and ran out of the church, stopping to put 50p in the collection box.

As luck would have it Geraldine's three brothers did manage to save the coffin from landing on the floor, but the wreath on the top of it they couldn't save. It went sliding off the coffin along the pedestal and off the other side, landing on its end in front of the altar. One of the brothers retrieved the battered wreath, which was supposed to say *SANDRA* but now said *SAND*. The *RA* had scooted underneath the altar. But we all said afterwards that *SAND* was not inappropriate because Sandra had got a caravan right near the beach at Scarborough.

Well Baz, in his semi-drunken state, burst out laughing. Him laughing, but trying not to, made this funny squeaking noise. This set Rose off laughing, then Cheryl, then me, and before long most of the mourners was laughing. We just couldn't stop. Handkerchiefs were being shoved into mouths throughout the congregation.

Father Pickles had no choice but to stop the service, and he sent Baz outside for a fag. Then when everybody had calmed down he restarted it. It was horrendous; so disrespectful. It was just one of those times when you lose control, so embarrassing, it was.

Father Pickles then had to rush the service after the delay, because the next funeral had already arrived and was waiting outside in the blooming rain. Sandra's coffin didn't half go fast down that burial hole.

Geraldine wouldn't stay for her mother's wake, she had the narks on with everybody. I rang her later. She said she was sure the scream came from the coffin, from her mother. I tried to console her.

I told her if it was her mother screaming I'm sure she would have screamed again when they plunged her at speed into that grave. I'm surprised we didn't hear her head hitting the coffin lid. Sandra was frightened to death of lifts and escalators when she was alive – not so much going up, but going down was hell for her. If she was still alive she would have screamed alright, loud and clear. I think that put Geraldine's mind at rest.

I bet she gave Baz a right bollocking.

BARRY

My Marks and Sparks interview today, and what a right blooming day it was.

Got up, was giving my teeth a good brush and my top front crown came out, leaving this pointed thing. I looked like a bloody vampire.

I knew it was a bit loose and I've got an appointment at the dentist next week. I couldn't believe it – of all days for it to come out!

So I scrounged around looking for some Hard as Nails and couldn't find any – the only thing I could find was some cheap glue, so put it over the point and wedged the crown back on. It wasn't very secure but it looked okay.

Also, I'd forgotten to pick up my suit yesterday. Rushed out and they were shut due to flooding in the basement. All that rain we've had.

I had to go to the interview in my brown corduroy jacket, which looks a bit worn. The new blue striped shirt didn't go with it at all, so I wore my dark beige one and my brown tie.

The interview seemed to be going well. I answered all their questions intelligently, or so I thought. Then as I was telling them how many stores and staff they had, the crown came off and I nearly swallowed it. Well, I started to cough and splutter; I couldn't stop. I thought I was going to choke.

They fetched me some water, said, "Thank you for coming", and the interview ended, as quick as that.

What a mess. I was in there for about ten minutes, five of them choking. Hopefully the first five minutes went well. First interview in four months and then that happens. I've got that much on my mind organising these concerts that I'm letting other, more important things go. Get a grip, man. I better not mention it to Bev, she'll go barmy, and I don't blame her really. I could have got that job, I'm sure. I am a prat, that's what I am: a prat.

There's big trouble about the Saturday night big concerts. The women are right annoyed with us men. Just hope it all calms down.

There was a deputation from the ladies' section committee to the club committee, and of course our lass was there. They want us to reserve a table for them on the Saturday nights in the concert room. We told them we can't do that, it wouldn't work. Somebody would sit at it and if we tried to move them there'd just be trouble. And we don't want trouble.

Anyway, if we started that everybody would want to reserve a table and not turn up till nine o'clock, so where would that leave the bar takings?

Our lass got a bit shirty and for some reason, I haven't got a clue why, and in front of everyone, I got pulled over the coals for forgetting to get some ham in for her tea, leaving my empty cup in the lounge and not folding the tea towel over the oven door. She scoots all over the bloody place. What's boiled ham, cups and tea towels got to do with the Saturday concerts? Everybody was looking at her as though she was daft.

Cheryl brought us back to the subject in question by saying if we don't reserve them a table then the women want to go into the Men Only, but only after it's had a good fettle. I must admit it's a bit grubby in there, but I know for a fact that the club finances won't stretch to having it decorated.

The ladies left and the committee discussed it. Some of the oldies said it was the thin end of the wedge. They didn't want women in the Men Only, full stop. In the end the committee voted four to eight against. It's not easy, not easy. Why is life such a bloody pain?

BEV

Called in to see Connie, and she had a little cry about her sister. She said she hadn't seen her in nine years. But they had kept in regular touch with each other by phone; that is until her sister became stone deaf six years ago!

I said either me or Barry would take her to the funeral, and she was pleased about that. Bless her. To be old and alone, eh?

Called in at Cheryl's on my way to work. I put my foot right in it. I am a big mouth. She was going on about Ralph's ex-wife Donna who lives on her own with

Ralph's thirteen-year-old son Denver – that's where he was conceived, in Denver, Colorado. Ralph and Donna were on honeymoon there. Well, Donna is ringing Ralph for the least little thing and to Cheryl's annoyance Ralph goes running. It makes Cheryl's blood boil. Ralph says it's to keep the peace, because Donna once threatened to stop him seeing Denver. She is a spiteful woman.

Apparently she rang Ralph last night because Denver fancied a McDonald's and Donna couldn't go because she had to look after him. He didn't feel very well. He'd got an upset tummy.

"He wants a McDonald's and he's got a tummy upset, really?" Cheryl said sarcastically, her eyes going heavenward.

They do put on Ralph and he takes it, which infuriates Cheryl. So, me big gob brought it up about Ralph being arrested and in prison overnight for bashing a bloke who he found in bed with Donna while they were still married. Well, Cheryl knew nothing about it. She went white. They'll be ructions when Ralph gets in from work. I didn't know she didn't know. I thought everybody knew.

I changed the subject to my new butterfly top. She wasn't interested; she was deep in thought. So I supped my tea and made a quick exit.

Went to work in my new pink and navy uniform and the boss never said a word. She noticed, though, because she had me cleaning all the shelves. Maureen, who works mornings, usually does that. Maureen has got a very unfortunate face; in fact, bless her, she's so blooming ugly that the boss tries to keep her away from the counter and the customers as much as possible. I suppose it could be off-putting to some folk because we sell sandwiches as well as other food stuff.

27

Rose has got her first date with a fella called Alan; she is over the moon.

BARRY

I signed on the dole today. Looked through the jobs but there was nothing. Dennis told me he'd heard they were taking folks on at the sausage factory. I'll have to pop in. Be good if I got a job there; I could walk it there and back every day, save on bus fares. Bev says it's not bad wages either and that beggars can't be choosers. She's right I suppose, better a menial job than no job. Making sausages, eh? A bit different to engineering! Although I suppose you could say you have to engineer the sausage meat into the sausage skin.

I didn't tell Bev when I was first made redundant. I couldn't, somehow. I went out every morning as though I was going to work, pack up the lot.

What am I doing? I thought. *This is bloody ridiculous.* So I told her and she was fine about it, very supportive. She was more upset that I couldn't bring myself to tell her. We've always been truthful with each other.

"Don't worry, you'll soon get another job – you've got lots of experience," she said.

But as the weeks, then months, went by she started accusing me of not trying. I'm bloody trying, I really am. I've shown Bev every application I've sent off to let her know I am trying. But she is up and down. One minute she is sympathetic, next she's angry, and as time goes on, she is getting more angry and less sympathetic, and I'm getting more dejected. I need a job.

If I hadn't got the club to concentrate on I think I would have done myself in.

The variety agent has sent us the name of the act for next Saturday. Cheese and Onion, comedy vocal duo. I'm going to get ads in the local papers; see if we can pull them in like last Saturday. If I leave it to Sam it'll not get done. Finger crossed.

BEV

Had a long confab with Cheryl. The lasses are all livid about this business at the club. They've left us nowhere to go. Cheryl wants to call a meeting of the ladies' section tomorrow before the line dancing see what we can come up with.

She's been going on at me about my cholesterol levels, can you believe? She's getting like my mother used to be. Because I was eating a couple of – well, three – Walnut Whips. I told her to mind her own business. I need some pleasure in my life. That bloody husband of mine doesn't give me any. Sex is a thing of the past with us.

I called in to see Rose; asked her about her date with Alan. She said he was nicely built, very smart, nice jacket, nice shirt, nice face, but his fingernails were dead mucky. Then she said as they were eating their rhubarb crumble she learned he had thirty-nine hanging baskets.

"Thirty-nine hanging baskets?" I said. I couldn't stop laughing. She said she didn't know whether to buy him a pair of gardening gloves, or pack him. By the time they were on to their coffee she'd decided to pack him. The thought of them dirty fingernails touching her body made her want to vomit. She's looking for the next one now.

BARRY

Me and our lass have had a big blowout. She thinks because I'm the club secretary I can just sort it. She can't get it in her head that the committee make the rules, not me. I just put them into practice. I told her it wouldn't bother me, the women going into the Men Only, but it's not my call. You can't just change an eighty-odd-year-old tradition at the flip of a cap.

That Men Only room has been there since the club was built in 1932. Women have never wanted to go in there before, so that's how it's stayed. Nobody questioned it. I know in this day and age it sounds sexist, but that's how it is. I know it needs changing, but it can't be changed in a day, there are procedures to go through.

Course, it came up what usually comes up when she's ranting. When am I going to get a job? Doesn't matter what we row about, that always comes up. I wish I could get a flaming job, woman!

She so resents the fact that she's working and I'm not. I really do wish it was the other way around. She seems to think I can just walk out of the house and come back with a job. Good God, woman, I wish it was that easy.

She threw a wet dishcloth at me. It came at a right speed. They bloody hurt, wet dishcloths, as opposed to dry dishcloths. Missed me by inches and smashed into the clock, which went flying off the wall on to the table, sending three cups crashing to the floor. Thank God for Poundland.

When that woman of mine is angry, she goes barmy. It could have taken my eye out, that dishcloth. I couldn't stand it anymore; I legged it, quickly.

She threw the sweeping brush at me as I'm heading down the garden path. I tripped over it and fell into the flaming privet hedge. Getting yourself out of the middle of a five-foot-high privet hedge is not easy, not easy at all. I've got scratches all over my hands and face to prove it. I could have had my blooming eye out. Course, she thought me scrabbling about in the privet was hilarious. Fell about laughing, she did. As did Mable and Gladys; they were parked on their scooters outside the house, eating battered sausages. Just blatantly listening to us two going at it. Not a bit embarrassed. They'll have scooted to the club with all the gossip. Still, while they are talking about us, they're leaving some other bugger alone.

Oh, for a peaceful life.

31

BEV

The meeting went very well. There were fifty-nine women attended. Even some of them that didn't line dance came. Cheryl took the chair. She's right good at that sort of thing. It was all done proper. We put it to the vote. The decision was that we are not standing for it. The club is our social life as well as the men's and we ought to have a say. So we've decided to get a petition up. We only want to sit in the Men Only on a Saturday; it's not too much to ask. Geraldine is having some leaflets and stickers printed at work.

We understand that the club is in financial difficulty. But if we can't get a seat in the concert room and there are spare seats in the Men Only, common sense says we should be allowed to sit in them; it's all money going over the bar. Never mind the old fogies and their rule number fifty-seven.

Emergency at work today: this bloke came in, took an armful of goods, then went out and drove off without paying for his petrol or the goods. He weren't young either, smart suit, nice big expensive car, not the type you would expect to do a runner. He took three growbags and a bottle of red wine and his petrol came to over sixty quid.

Anyway, we sent for the police. This middle-aged inspector, uniformed, and this younger lad copper came. They arrived within about three hours; not bad going these days. He was gorgeous – the inspector, not the young copper. He'd got short, pure white hair and he was nicely tanned. Wearing a pristine white shirt that matched his hair. And them uniforms – wow.

He was asking me questions and I could hardly answer him. I was like a blooming daft teenager. He asked for the security camera footage. I told him the camera isn't working. He pulled a face at that, but he was still handsome. All the time I'm thinking, *Oh, I bet my face is all shiny, mi nose especially*. At that time of the day I look like I've been sprayed with some WD40. I must have looked and sounded right stupid. I was all giggling and talking rubbish.

I think he got fed up with me in the end, because he started asking the boss all the questions. Of course she was very articulate. I'm sure she's gay. The inspector told us there wasn't much they could do, but we should get the security camera working.

BARRY

Brilliant night again. Bar takings well up. We'd put a £2 charge on the door, except for the regular members; doorman let them in for nothing. We'd put the beer up 2p a pint, and none of our lot noticed, or if they did they didn't say anything. Cheese and Onion, yes, we'll have them back.

The women were outside the club with their petition, getting signatures from anybody that would sign. Charlie and Albert wanted to move them off, which would have escalated the trouble. So I was glad they were just off the club premises so we couldn't say anything.

I've talked to a lot of the blokes, and most of them think

the Men Only should stay as it is – them that frequent the Men Only, that is.

Old Charlie said they wouldn't be able to swear anymore with the ladies in there. He should come to our house and hear what our lass can turn out. Also, the women would make an issue about farting. Albert said he wasn't going to the bog every time he wanted to fart, not at his age and with his bad legs. He said he'd be in and out of the bog all night, with his bowels.

Charlie said he knew a bloke whose wife wouldn't let him fart and it killed him. Blew him up like a balloon, crushed all his organs. As soon as he died all the air that he'd been holding in expelled itself, and although he died laid on the settee in the lounge, the backdraught fired him into the kitchen. He hit the wall and exploded. Could hear it miles away, he said. The police came; they thought it was a terrorist attack. The undertaker had to collect up all the pieces, his wife was too distressed.

They are a pair of lying barmpots, them two. They're both coming up with these blooming daft stories and reasons why we shouldn't let the women in the Men Only. They think I've fell off the blooming Christmas tree. Death by fart! I bet that's a new one on the death certificate.

Oh, for a peaceful life. I feel like a piece of ham squashed between two slices of bread.

BEV

We had a right laugh collecting signatures outside the club. We put up a little gazebo in case it rained, but it didn't. We had a small table, chairs and a stove to brew some tea, and a few bottles of red wine.

Rose fetched some fish and chips across; it was like going camping. Actually, it was better than being in the club. We were giggling at anything anybody said. We were like a bunch of teenage lasses.

It was all good-natured – a few of the men gave us some backchat, but we really enjoyed it. Got loads of signatures from the women, some of them not even local, and a few men even signed.

At one point we started chanting our version of Winston Churchill's speech:

We will fight them in the concert room.
We will fight them in the lobby.
We will fight them in the car park.
We will never surrender.

Then Slimy Sam came out and said that the turn wanted us to be quiet as we were spoiling their act, so we shut up.

Geraldine got a load of signatures from the church. Father Pickles was fine about her asking the parishioners.

But she told us that when she was cleaning the church today, apparently Father Pickles has asked her and some of the other women to give it a good fettle because the bishop is visiting next week. They're doing all the brasses and polishing the pews and what have you.

She said Baz came marching into the church effing and blinding because when he'd called for some petrol today, whilst the boss was taking his money I sneaked out and stuck a sticker on the back of his cab, and he's been picking

35

up fares all day with a *Women for the Men Only* sticker on his back side window.

He knew that it would be Geraldine that had had them printed at work, and he knew that it would be me that had stuck it on his car. She said he called us things she can't repeat.

He said Old Charlie sarcastically brought the sticker to his attention. So everybody in the club will know about it now, and him a committee man at that. He'll not be able to hold his head up.

Geraldine said he was absolutely fuming, and as he left the church he shouted at the top of his voice, "And yer can tell yer Father bloody Pickles to shove his bishop's visit up his fucking cassock."

He's never liked her involvement with the church.

She said it echoed all around the church, then she said Father Pickles appeared from behind a pillar, all flustered and rushed, nearly falling his full length into the vestry, wiping his eyes. She just wanted to die. Father Pickles has got noticeably big feet, I seen him trip up many a time.

She said everybody carried on with their polishing as though nothing had happened, except Cynthia Celia, she was smirking. She's hated Geraldine ever since that time she overheard Geraldine tell Mary that Father Pickles would make a good primate. Cynthia accused Geraldine of calling him a monkey and told Father Pickles, who had to explain to Cynthia that a primate is another name for an archbishop. Cynthia hasn't spoken to Geraldine since, and Geraldine is certain it's Cynthia that's pinched her Cillit Bang.

It was the worst day of her life, she said.

He is a vulgar man though, Baz. He's not talking to me now, but who's bothered?

BARRY

Took Connie to her sister's funeral, and would you believe it, there were only six folk there – sad. Brought her back and sat with her for a while. She was telling me about when they were young, during the war. Every night whether the sirens went off or not, her mother would make them go into the Anderson shelter. Her sister, who died, finished up with elephantiasis with the damp; her legs swelled up to the size of two. We haven't got a clue what they all went through in that war.

I thought, we're letting these old, war-torn folk die off without listening to all their stories. Stories about what ordinary folk went through. It's over seventy years ago now, the Second World War. They'll all have gone soon and it'll be too late, we'll have missed it.

Bev left me a note to give the kitchen a good clean today, and what did I find hidden in the top cupboard? Hoards of chocolates, sweets – all sorts of stuff. She must have forgotten about them, the 'use by' dates are out. I've slung them.

The menu she's made out for the week is all salads. She's thrown all the butter in the bin; no more butter in the house, she says. What about me, eh? I like butter on mi bread. I think she thinks there's only her lives here.

Our Julie rang. "Dad, can you lend me five hundred

quid? My car's had it, and I've got chance of this second-hand Skoda. I've got to have something for the school run." She knows if she mentions the kids she'll get it. She still owes me two hundred quid from last Christmas.

I'm not kidding, her and her mother think my redundancy money's going to last forever. Got my tooth fixed – £300, scandalous. Then £500 for our Julie, that's £800 in one day. Money goes nowhere these days.

I nipped into the job centre, nothing again.

Can you believe it, there was a reporter from the *Evening Star* waiting outside the club for me today, asking about the Men Only skirmish with the women. I told him in no uncertain terms where to go, but later I did see him interviewing Charlie and Albert, and they were really giving it some mouth.

BEV

What a day today was. I am still buzzing about it.

I was just giving this man his change, when this heavily pregnant young woman came rushing in shouting, "Help me, I'm in labour. I think I can feel it coming."

Well, it was panic stations. We got her a chair.

The boss shouted, "Is there a doctor in the house?"

Of course there wasn't. One man shouted, "I'm a plumber." Don't know what good he thought that was.

Geoff rushed off to call for an ambulance. Geoff is retired; he comes in one day a week to do some of the odd jobs.

She said, "I think I need to take my knickers off."

"Not in here, love!" I croaked – well, there was a shop full of men. "We had better go through to the back," I said. Which we did; bless her, she could hardly walk.

The boss wasn't much help either. She said, in her frantic, high-pitched 'Oh my God, what is happening?' voice, "You see to her, I can't – I'm not a midwife. I'll carry on serving."

I'm not a midwife either, yer daft bat, I thought.

I was terrified, I was, and so was this poor lass. I'm praying, *Please, God, do not let this woman give birth here, because I will probably faint.*

Her pains were coming every few seconds, or so it seemed. Only thing I could think of doing was to make a cup of tea.

She said, "Have you delivered any babies before?"

I said, "No, sorry, I'm afraid I h—"

She didn't let me finish. She burst into tears. "I want mi mam," she sobbed.

I jumped in. "But some years ago, I did help deliver three baby hamsters," I said.

That information didn't seem to allay her fears. She sobbed even louder.

I do not want to deliver this baby, I thought.

Then – thank God, he must have heard my prayers – I could hear the ambulance siren in the distance. We looked at each other and we both gave a sigh of relief.

I nearly delivered a baby this morning.
This woman rushed in and without any warning
Shouted and screamed, "I'm about to give birth!"
She'd filled up her tank forty quid's worth.

The boss looked like she was going to be sick.
And Geoff, he just stood about like a prick.
It was all left to me; I tried not to panic.
She grabbed for a chair. The place was just manic.

Customers queuing, their tanks full of fuel.
This poor frightened lass. Gosh, life can be cruel.
It's okay in a manger, surrounded by livestock.
But a garage? Poor kid, she must be in right shock.

The ambulance came, we all gave a sigh.
We all of us flopped as we waved her goodbye.
She shouts, "What's your name?" I shouted back, "Bev."
"They've said it's a boy, so his name will be Trev."

Wasn't that nice of her? I hope she brings the baby in to show us. I didn't half cry when she'd gone; relief, I think. Barbara gave me a Mars bar. I needed it – my sugar levels were at an all-time low.

BARRY

Gave the house a really good clean this morning, it's not fair to expect Bev to do any when I'm not working. I don't think I do it good enough for her, though. She won't let me do the washing; that's her domain. I do my own ironing. I hate ironing.

Can't wait to see what Charlie and Albert had to say to

that bloody reporter. It'll not be anything good, knowing them two. They are the bane of this club. They think because they are the oldest members they can run the bloody place. We will just have to wait and see.

BEV

Us lasses can't believe it, it's gobsmacking, what them two old gits Charlie and Albert have said about us women in the newspaper. I'm horrified, I am – we all are. Who do they think they are?

Apparently they said that our women's brains would be bored stiff when Charlie and Albert and their colleagues are discussing world politics, economics, global warming and the state of the planet.

The prats! Only thing I've ever heard that lot discuss is football, food, fishing and f…flu jabs. They are silly old codgers. There's going to be big, big trouble, I reckon.

Rose has a date. Nick, he's a schoolteacher. Hope his fingernails are clean.

We've got a different supplier at the garage now and he brought these wonderful, gorgeous, scrumptious fresh cream cakes. Oh my god, how I'm going to keep my hands off them, I don't know. My mouth waters every time I walk past the cold counter. If I seriously want to lose weight I need to get another job. Perhaps a traffic warden, or a till operator at the local B&Q? No – till operator's no good; it's a very sedentary occupation.

Come to think of it, I am on the go most of the time at the garage, no time for sitting with the boss on my back. So perhaps it's not such a bad job after all. The amount of calories I use running around would certainly allow for one cream cake. That's it then, one cream cake every day. Problem sorted.

Cheryl was fuming today. Her and Ralph had been to Sainsbury's for their weekly shop and when they had loaded the car, Ralph's son Denver came running over. Donna, the detested ex-wife, had run out of petrol in Sainsbury's car park, silly bitch. So Ralph went to help her and Cheryl went home in a mood with the groceries.

As Cheryl was unloading the car, she tripped and fell over Denver's skateboard that he'd left parked on their doorstep.

Other than a twisted knee, bruising to her forehead where she'd hit the door frame trying unsuccessfully to save the wine bottles she was carrying, and a badly bruised wrist, she didn't do much damage to herself. But she was bloomin' fuming about the four bottles of wine she'd smashed, and the time she spent at the hospital getting an X-ray of her knee.

"Twenty-four quid, the wine cost," she ranted. "Just because his bloody stupid ex can't be bothered to put some petrol in her car." She was ever so mad.

I thought the bruising on her forehead might turn into a black eye. But I didn't voice my suspicions – you could tell she felt bad enough.

BARRY

Well thank you, Albert and Charlie, your interview in the *Evening Star* was brilliant. It will really help the peace along. Flaming reporters.

Our Julie called up – she's got the car, but she asked for another £200 to get it through its test. Kids, they never stop costing you – she's twenty-four and I'm still having to dig deep into my pocket for her. I can't remember mine or Bev's parents forking out for us. I suppose they hadn't got much spare cash in them days. My dad was a builder's labourer and my mother was a cleaner at the local secondary school. Not big wages, but they managed and they were happy.

I went for a walk down the woods. I do love it down there. I saw that squirrel again. Well, I think it's the same one. I stood still and it came right up to me this time, it's not a bit frightened. They must be able to sense whether you're hostile or not. It looked me right in the eye. I bent down and it ran off, it wasn't taking any chances. I'm not sure whether squirrels are vermin or not; must look it up.

With all the rain we've had everything is lush and green. All the different greens, they're really beautiful. I wish I was an artist. I've got the most wonderful subject right here on my own doorstep.

BEV

Geraldine brought a pile of magazines round for me, and there's this diet where you can lose half a stone in four days. It's all the rage in Hollywood. You eat nothing but jars of baby food. I'm going to nip to Sainsbury's to get some. I used to like them when our Julie was little – a spoonful for her, then a spoonful for me. No wonder she's only five foot one and eight stone. Poor kid must have been malnourished!

We got 906 signatures on our petition. Rose had a petition in the chippy, and we got over two hundred from there. She said she bribed them with a few extra chips. I was asking the women drivers to sign when they were buying their petrol. We stood outside the local Sainsbury's and got loads from there until this manager-type bloke came out and told us to move on.

I shouted at him, "Hey, we do our shopping here, mate, and I've just bought twenty-four jars of baby food." He still moved us on. So we went and stood outside the Co-op.

Cheryl didn't come with us. She says she is staying indoors while her eye is black, although she says it's a light purple now.

We did everything we could think of, so we were in a right good mood when we went to the office to hand in the petition.

Then in between the bingo and the raffle, Slimy Sam came onstage and announced that the petition was not legal as it wasn't sponsored by the committee. For it to count in any way, shape or form the signees must be full members, and full members are men.

We were right angry. Where do we go from here?

Hope Cheryl thinks of something, she's the one with the brains. Her Ralph is on our side – he doesn't know it but he's our mole. He tells Cheryl everything that's said at the committee meetings; then she tells us. He says no matter how many times the committee put it to a vote, there's still that hard core of oldies that sees it as the thin end of the wedge.

Later, as we were leaving, Albert and Charlie were in the car park going barmy. Somebody had sprayed *PIG* in red paint on the tyres of their scooters. We couldn't stop laughing.

Albert looked at us. I said, "Don't you look at us, we haven't done it." But I commend them that did.

It serves them right. They're a pair of dinosaurs. Oh, aren't I awful?

BARRY

Bev hasn't said anything about the decision at the club. It might be because it's my birthday. To be honest I expected a big blow-up; I don't know what's happened there.

I didn't get a card from her. I got one from our Julie, Dan and the boys. She put on it, *Sorry, Dad, couldn't afford to get you a pressie – the lads need some new shoes, and I'm skint.* She's a cheeky beggar – she knows if she puts that I'll give her the money for the shoes. Kids, eh? I'll ring her.

Bev has always insisted that she does all the washing, but I noticed all my stuff was still left in the basket, so she's definitely mad at me.

A nice birthday present would be for me to get a job.

I've surpassed myself today: I have written a poem. I think it must be the very first time I've ever written one.

Hey, little squirrel, come to me
You move as fast as a flying bee
Don't worry, I'm not here to harm
So please, let us both be calm

We're so very different, you and I
But both God's creatures under the sky
I want to get to know you, chum
I want to see just how you've done

So please don't run away from me
Don't rush away like a buzzing bee
Let us be friends, let us both share
A moment together, showing we care

I'll see you again, my little friend
Please don't let our friendship end
So goodbye and thanks for being here
I think it's time I went for a beer
See you soon

BEV

It's Barry's birthday today. I'd already got a card that I bought last year and didn't give him. I didn't give it him again this year. Well, what could I possibly write on it? *Love you, you lousy chauvinist pig*?

Tried the baby food – they are nice but one jar's no good. I had four for my dinner.

Went to Cheryl's for a cuppa to see if she had any thoughts about the situation us women find ourselves in. I'm glad to say her black eye is no longer black; it's a light purple/brown. Rose and Geraldine were there.

Cheryl said, "Seeing as the men insist that the signees on the petition have to be full members, then perhaps that is what we should aim for. Full membership for the women."

We all thought it was brilliant. Full membership, yes, why not?

She always comes up with something, does Cheryl – she got some O and A Levels, she is very clever.

She offered us some cake, and I hummed and ha'd a bit, then said yes. Well, I might know that started me off – called at the shop, got some cake, biscuits and a big bar of Fruit & Nut. Felt guilty but had to eat them because it would be wasteful not to.

Rose's date with Nick the schoolteacher went arse upwards. He's married and just wants a bit on the side. He said he would pay for their nights out if she would let him have sex. She said she was sat with an empty glass half the night.

She said, "I only had three halves of lager. I'm worth more than £4.50. And the cheeky bastard wanted to take me to my work for some chips, because of my discount. I told him to bugger off."

She's not seeing him again. I told her she wants to watch it. She said not to worry; she always leaves their names and phone numbers on the coffee table in case she gets murdered.

"Oh, great. That's alright then," I said.

She says she knows her soulmate is out there somewhere – she just has to find him. I hope she does, I really hope she does.

Sat and watched Gerard Butler in *Phantom*. I can watch it over and over. Then I felt bloated and sick. Must have been the baby food.

BARRY

Do they never stop, these women? They have now handed the committee a demand for full membership or they will boycott the club and take their custom to The Blue Bell. I told the committee we need the women's custom. What good is making money on the Saturday concert if we lose money the rest of the week?

Sam said, "We could have strippers on every Sunday dinnertime. That would bring some extra punters in."

"Aye, it would – the dirty mac brigade."

He'd love that, him, having strippers on, being the concert secretary. He'd use it as a bit of status, to nip in and out of the dressing room and see if he could catch them naked. The women call him a slimy git, and they're not wrong.

Then Baz pointed out that if the women get full membership, they can be voted on to the committee.

That shocked us all, even me. It's something none of us had thought about. I'm all for letting them go in the Men Only and getting full membership, but women on the committee is another kettle of fish altogether.

Dennis said, "A mixed-sex committee would never be able to agree on anything."

I think he's dead right there. Things are getting so complicated.

After much discussion the consensus was that they'd end up running the club like they do the home.

Albert, the daft beggar, said, "Them women, they'd want tablecloths, curtains, doilies, fancy wallpaper, and most important of all, *NO FARTING* signs up, even in the gents'." He's obsessed with his freedom to fart, that man.

Charlie put his spoke in and said, "We must fight. The Alamo, Custer's last stand, the Zulus – men died for what they believe in, brave men. The women were just there to load the guns."

I think them two are having us on. They do talk some rubbish.

I said, "I don't think we'd die, Charlie, but the club might."

They reckon you get dafter as you get older – Albert and Charlie certainly have. I think they are secretly enjoying all this; it puts a bit of drama into their lives. But it could be very dangerous for the club.

The pressure is on. It's too big a decision for the committee alone to decide. I think we are going to have to put it to a full members' vote.

If the women got full membership, I'm sure Bev would want to be on the committee, she wouldn't be able to help herself. It would be hell. Bev on the committee – I'd feel like cutting my throat. I started to question myself then. Am I a male chauvinist? I've never considered myself to be one, I've always considered myself to be an enlightened man. But I'm doubtful now, with what's going on inside my head.

That bloody reporter was outside the club again, pestering folk for information. He is getting to be a blooming nuisance – I wish he would step on to the club premises. Then I could tell him to sling his hook. But he cleverly makes sure he stays on the public footpath where we have no jurisdiction, clever sod. Step out of line, mate, and I'll have you.

BEV

Geraldine called in this morning in a huff. Her and Baz had been shopping in Crystal Peaks and they were looking in the jewellers' window. She said they had some beautiful stuff. She particularly liked a pair of silver earrings and she made sure Baz knew how much she liked them – it's their wedding anniversary next week. Anyway, when they got home Baz said he'd got to go back as he'd forgotten something. She was sure he'd gone back to buy her the earrings.

"He was ages," she said.

After a while she couldn't contain herself, so she rang him. "Where are you?"

"Well, you know that jewellers you were looking in?" he said. "I'm in the betting shop next door."

"I could brain him. The miserly git," she growled. She was as mad when she left as when she arrived – it'll take her days to get over it. She does make me laugh.

I think I have done my back in at work today. I'm in right pain. This little old lady came in; she must have been ninety. She was extremely well-dressed and well-spoken, pronounced all her aitches and spoke with elongated vowels. You know, 'barth' for 'bath', 'graaarse' for 'grass', 'cart' for 'cat', that sort of thing.

Well, she wanted twenty growbags. I shouted for Geoff, it was his day to come in and he usually does things like that, but he didn't answer. I think he must have been round the back having a fag.

So the boss told me to load them into the wagon. If I didn't need my job so much I would have told her, "Up yours."

I was puffing and panting, I mean, twenty growbags? I could feel my sugar levels dropping down to my feet.

When I'd finished loading them, the old woman smiled, winked, and pressed 50p into my palm. Then the cheeky old beggar said, "I always use Deep Heat, it's very good for a bad back."

She may be a little old lady, she may be over ninety. She may talk posh. But at that moment I just wanted to smash her little old face in.

Hope to God she doesn't come back for more or it will be "Up yours, missus."

BARRY

Bev's done her back in at work. She's in a foul mood. I don't want to make her worse. I've had to fetch her some Deep Heat and some painkillers from the chemist. She's now laid out on the settee reading romantic novels – she buys loads of them. I think that's one of our problems: she expects me to live up to all these bloody heroes she reads about.

BEV

The ladies' section committee went to meet the club committee in the office tonight. Much to our chagrin, the men have made their decision. They have voted to stay with the status quo; in other words, they don't want women as full members. We would want to be on the committee, they say. We told them we don't want to be on the committee.

"Some woman, one day, would," they said. If it's good enough for the church to fight against having women bishops, then it is good enough for them not to have women committee persons, they told us.

Cheryl promptly updated them. "Well, if you lot kept up with the news, you would know that they do have women bishops now," she said.

Baz came back swiftly, "Then they're bloody crackers, and it is not illegal."

We left the office and went to have a meeting in The Bell; we didn't want the men eavesdropping.

Right, so they won't let us go in the Men Only and they don't want us as full members. We agreed we've got to fight this. They're treating us as though we are some lower beings. Second-class citizens. This is the twenty-first century, not the Middle Ages.

Geraldine says that Baz says she's suffering from PMT. She told him, "Yes, you lot: prats, morons and twits."

Cheryl corrected her. "It's called PMS now," she said.

"Okay then – prats, morons and…shits."

She says she's withdrawn all sex from Baz, after the 'bishop up yer effing cassock' and the silver earring do. She said she can't even bear to look at him after what he put her through in that church. Cynthia Celia smirks at her every time she sees her and the other women look at her all pitiful. She hates Baz at the moment. She called him a horrible gobshite.

She said she threw his dinner at him and the bastard ducked. Egg and beans embedded in the wallpaper. She told him she wasn't cleaning it up. When she got back from work, he'd sprayed it with varnish, put a picture frame around it and called it *Passion Food*.

BARRY

The local radio station have asked representatives from both the men and the women to go on the radio. We weren't keen but the women jumped at the chance, so we had better send somebody.

I definitely don't want to go. There's only Dennis and Sam that's volunteered. They're not the brightest pair in the bunch. We'll have to see.

I went up to the sausage factory today. They asked me if I liked sausage! Didn't know what answer they expected for that. I said, "Aye", because I do. Anyway, I've filled a form in. We'll see.

Saw my squirrel again. I'd taken a bit of bread to give it, but it stuck its nose up. It looked at me as if to say, *Is that all you've brought?* Then it ran up a tree; they can't half motor up them trees. I'm a bit ignorant about squirrels, I'll have to look them up on the internet and see what they eat. It's probably carrots.

BEV

Oh, I'm so excited – me and Cheryl are going to be on the local radio. I'm going to wear my butterfly sequinned top. I know the listeners can't see you, but it makes me feel good.

Cheryl's picking me up at half past ten. I've never been on the radio before. Oh, I tell a lie, I was on when Princess

Di came to Sheffield. They were interviewing people in the crowd. They asked what I thought of her

"Lovely," I said.

The radio station have advertised it as the battle of the sexes at the Kenthorpe Miners' Welfare club. I can't believe it we're famous.

11.30pm

Cheryl was brilliant today at the radio station. Articulate, bright, to the point.

When Dozy Dennis said the club didn't need the women, she replied that the women are responsible for 35% of the takings in the club. I don't know where she got that information from. She might have made it up for all I know, but it sounded good. He didn't know how to answer it anyway, so he stuttered out that we were a bunch of pudding burners, daft sod.

I responded quickly and bluntly with, "I have never burnt a pudding in my life." I felt dead daft after I'd said it. I thought, *What did I say that for? Daft beggar. I burnt one on Sunday.*

Dennis said, "Would the Women's Institute have men on their committees?"

"No," Cheryl said, "because the Women's Institute does not need men, but the club does need women."

Then Slimy Sam got a piece of paper from his pocket, got it all written down, he had. I bet his mother had done it for him.

He said, "Women are equal to men, of course."

Big deal, bastard, I thought.

He went on, "But in theory some jobs are for men and some for women. Being on the committee of a working men's club is a man's job, as it says in the title, 'working men'."

I said, "Well, half of you aren't working. Half of you are on the dole."

I was going to say, 'bloody dole', but I stopped myself (radio).

He ignored me and then gave an example of a woman doing a man's job.

"A big fat man is on the nineteenth floor of a hotel. His life is in danger because the hotel is on fire. And who comes up the ladder to rescue him? A nine-stone scraggy woman firefighter. I think at this point any man would change their mind about the automatic equality of the sexes," he said. "Because she is going to drop you, isn't she?"

He looked straight at Cheryl. He'd thought he'd scored a point with that one.

The interviewer looked quite impressed.

Then Cheryl said, very profoundly and looking Slimy Sam straight in the face, "A fireman's ladder does not reach the nineteenth floor."

Slimy Sam looked gutted; she'd undercut him.

After that the interview just got more and more hyper and ended up with a slanging match between me and Slimy Sam.

I called him a twisted git.

He called me a big fat elephant.

Calling me fat on the radio – I was absolutely fuming. The folk that were listening wouldn't have known I was fat till that prat said it.

I couldn't stop myself. I went for him. He tried to get away and the silly sod tripped over some cables and fell prostrate across the blooming table, knocking all the drinks over. Me and Cheryl laughed at first, but the liquid must have leaked into the electronics. They have too many wires in them places.

The next thing we heard this sizzling, and then things like blue streaks of lightning started shooting around the room. It was terrifying. (BBC cuts for you: get rid of the electricians, keep the executives.) We all dived under the table, except the interviewer. Don't know where he vanished to.

Sparks were flying all over, shooting all over in fact, like stacks of Roman candles, all going off at once. Then smoke appeared.

The fire alarms were deafening us; we had to shout to each other to be heard. The smoke was now affecting our breathing, and I knew I had to do something, or we would all die. They weren't much use, the blokes.

I moved out from under the table into the room, sparks flying all around me. I was risking my life, I knew that, but I needed to wet these tissues with the water that had been spilt on the table. I'd read in a book that if you put something wet over your mouth and nose it helps you to breathe until you can be rescued.

I dipped the tissues into the water. But the blooming things just fell to pieces, they were rubbish. Poundland!

I dived back under the table. Cheryl had some tissues so we put them dry over our mouths instead. We had to give Dennis and Sam some, because they hadn't got any.

They just left us there – nobody bothered to come in and get us, the cowards. I think they'd all left the building when the fire alarm went off.

We could have been killed. It was terrifying.

Geraldine and Rose said that one minute they were listening to the interview on the radio and the next it just cut off. They thought that might have been to do with me swearing. They'd warned us not to swear. But when you get mad, well, you swear!

Good job it was a big table. We just huddled together underneath it, coughing and spluttering. Our eyes were all running with the effects of the smoke.

Dennis sounded like he was weeping. He had some lovely aftershave on.

I genuinely thought, *This is it, we are going to die*.

My life didn't flash before me and I wasn't travelling toward any white light. But I did start picturing my funeral in my head. Barry and our Julie holding each other up, distraught and sobbing with grief. Barry wishing he had cherished me more. The committee men, standing in salute as my coffin is carried into the church. Gracie Fields singing *Wish Me Luck As You Wave Me Goodbye*, the lively version with the men's forces choir as backing. Flowers covering the whole of the club's car park, hundreds of them. I hope there is a heaven, if it's only to be able to neb at my own funeral. And it's all that slimy git's fault, tripping over the bloody wires.

Anyway, after the sparks had died down, and the smoke had cleared a bit, which seemed like forever, these two big security blokes came in and escorted us out. No, actually they chucked us out. Not even a 'Sorry, are you alright?' – nothing.

I'm not listening to that station again. I smacked Slimy Sam in the car park. Nobody's calling me a fat elephant on the radio and getting away with it.

He screamed. He's a mardy-arse; threatened to call the police.

Then two fire engines arrived, so me and Cheryl just legged it to the car and set off for home. But we had to stop, we were so upset, so we went to a pub and had a roast dinner and a couple of lagers.

I think we could sue that radio station for dangerous involvement or something like that.

Fat, indeed. I am fat, I know it, but it's not up to that slimy git to broadcast it.

BARRY

Listened to the radio interview. Didn't realise when it suddenly shut off that the studio was on fire. They could have been burnt to death, all of them.

Bev's frightened to death of fire. Her aunts' house got on fire when she was a kid and she watched them bring out the family dog, Rover, dead – very traumatic for a ten-year-old.

When we've gone on holiday in the past, she always has to find the hotel fire escape before we unpack. She's been known to change rooms three times to get near the fire doors. And she won't go higher than the fifth floor – that's as far as the fire ladders go.

I gave Sam a right dressing-down; he had no right to call Bev what he did. She's given him a black eye, though. His mother, Gabby Annie, came into the club and had a right go at me. She called me all sorts.

I still haven't heard anything from Marks and Spencer's. Still, no news is good news, they say. I think I might give them a ring. They'll certainly remember me, coughing and spluttering.

BEV

Rule number eighty-two has reared its ugly head. It says in the club's rulebook that any member who assaults another member can be barred from the premises.

Slimy Sam has put it before the committee to get me barred for assaulting him. He's got a black eye and he says I've done his back in.

His mother, Gabby Annie, came to the house. She had a right go at me for hitting her son. She said he couldn't sleep with his back now, and his black eye is getting blacker by the day. She said I ought to be ashamed of myself, a big fat woman like me hitting a ten-stone man with a back problem.

I'm not a violent person but I had to hold myself back from smacking her like I smacked him.

I told her it was rubbish. He injured himself when he fell across the table at the radio station. In fact I think I saw his eye hit the top of the microphone.

That's my story and I'm sticking to it. Cheryl said she never saw me hit him.

She's a right one, Gabby Annie, she's a widow now and she's only got Slimy Sam and he's dead spoilt and a mardy-arse.

She once told me that she charged her husband for sex, and if he was skint, she'd lend him a fiver till payday. If you looked at her you couldn't help but think she was overpricing herself.

Anyway, if that so-called committee think I am going to apologise to that creep they have another think coming. So they'll just have to bar me.

BARRY

I came in from the club and Bev's sat on the settee, reading her Kindle and eating a bar of chocolate, glass of wine in her hand.

I stood looking at her. She stared back at me.

"What's up with you?" she said. "What are you staring at, the cat's mother?"

So I told her that I had gone through the club's rulebook, and found out that she can't be barred from the club using rule eighty-two because the assault had to take place on club premises. She gave me a sarcastic round of applause.

"What assault?" she said. "I didn't assault him. Ask Cheryl, she saw no assault take place, and she was with me all the time. I saw him hit his eye on the microphone as he fell across the table."

"Dennis said you hit him when you were in the car park."

"Oh, and you would sooner believe them than me and Cheryl? Anyway, who's bloody bothered?" she said. "Now can I carry on with my reading, smart-arse?"

She can be a vicious cow sometimes.

I am really trying my best to sort out these problems. I've got the bank on mi back; I've got the committee arguing. I'm trying to find work, which isn't easy. And the way Bev looks at me sometimes, I think she hates mi guts.

I'm bloody fed up.

Heard from the sausage factory. It was a no. Perhaps I didn't get it because I said I liked sausage; perhaps they thought I would be pinching it. I should have said I didn't like it.

BEV

Feel lousy today. I think I must be a bit traumatised from what happened at the radio interview. It's just sinking in – to think that we could have been burned to death or died of inhaling all that smoke! It was terrifying.

Cheryl phoned; she doesn't feel too good either, her chest feels tight and she's coughing. She said she's taking a sickie; I said so am I.

I've never told anybody this, but when my Aunty Doreen's house got on fire, it was my fault.

I saw my Aunty Doreen going to the local shops and I knew she always left the door unlocked. So I went in. She always had lots of chocolates and cakes for us kids. I've always had a sweet tooth. No, not just a sweet tooth, I am a greedy pig.

Our Rover, mi Aunty Doreen's dog, was laid on the settee and he ran to me so I was playing with him when

I saw me Aunty Doreen's cigarettes and matches on the table. So I had a try. It tasted horrible so I threw both the match and the cigarette in the waste bin, and went to get the chocolate.

I turned and I was terrified to see these flames coming from the waste bin. I didn't know what to do. I knew I shouldn't be there, so I ran out, slamming the door behind me, and I just ran and ran.

I ended up in the park. I just sat there shaking, not knowing what to do. I knew I'd be in right trouble. What had I done?

Then I heard the fire engines and I knew it was very serious.

I sat in the park all afternoon, crying my eyes out. I didn't want to go back, didn't know what I would find. What I'd done.

When I eventually did go back my dad had been looking for me, they'd been worried stiff. My mother was comforting my Aunty Doreen, she was sobbing. Nearly everything her and me Uncle George owned had gone up in flames.

And our Rover was dead. He was a lovely dog, followed me all over, I loved that dog and I killed him. I was devastated. We all were. I sobbed and sobbed and sobbed.

Everything they managed to salvage was put out on the front garden and covered up with some tarpaulin that Uncle George got from his works. There was the three-piece suite, although it was badly scorched, the kitchen table, one chair, a standard lamp, a small coffee table and numerous other bits and pieces.

The next morning it had gone, all of it pinched during the night. Some folk, eh? They want burning.

They buried our Rover in our back garden, because they didn't know where they were eventually going to live. They had to come and live with us for a while, until the council found them a new house. My Aunty Doreen blamed herself; she thought she must have thrown the match into the waste bin. She was devastated. I didn't say anything, I couldn't, I daren't, knowing what I'd done. I did everything I could to make them feel comfortable.

I found out later in my life that they had no insurance. I've carried all that guilt with me ever since. I couldn't even find the courage to tell my Aunty Doreen on her deathbed. Bloody coward, I am. I am a bad person, I must be.

BARRY

The women are boycotting the club. They've moved up to The Blue Bell. Clive the landlord will be happy for the extra custom. We will be well down on the general bar takings.

As far as full membership goes, I must admit that having Bev sat with me in a committee meeting would make me very nervous. I know her; any disagreements she'd take back home with her. I think I would pack up being on the committee if Bev was on it.

If I could just persuade the men that we should let the women in the Men Only – it would only be on a Saturday when the big concert's on. Then the women would hopefully drop this demand for full membership.

The concert room starts filling up from about 6.30 for the concert, and most of the women have been used to coming in between eight and nine. A lot of them have commitments, work, family, etc. Our lass doesn't finish work till eight.

I've tried talking to the committee, but there is still that hard core that do not want the women in the Men Only. They just can't see the seriousness of it. I think some of them have got some brain cells missing.

Charlie and Albert and the rest of their little gang are adamant. No women are going to spoil their Saturday nights out, with all their jabbering on about women's things. They've become more entrenched since their tyres were sprayed with red paint.

It's become a war of attrition. Nobody wants to give in.

We could cancel the concerts, but they've been very successful and financially it would put us back where we started and then the club would definitely close.

I've got to get these men and women to see eye to eye on what's good for the club.

This club has been the hub of the village since it was built. Wedding receptions, birthday parties, christenings, funerals are all held here. If this club closed the damage done to the social life of the village would be enormous.

If only they could see some sense.

Now for the good news: we've got butter back in the kitchen. Yes!

BEV

Couldn't believe what happened at work today. That bloke that pinched them goods and sixty pounds worth of petrol did the same again. We didn't notice him at first. Then I saw him out of the corner of my eye and there he was. He'd got sixty pounds worth of petrol again and this time he pinched a garden shovel.

The boss pushed me outside and told me to go and apprehend him.

"I'm not apprehending him, he might hit me with the bloody shovel," I said.

We sent for the police and that nice inspector came again. But he lost interest when he asked for the security camera footage and it still wasn't working.

"I got a bit of his number plate," I said. "Number two." He didn't bother to write it down.

The cheek of some folk, eh?

We had a great night in The Bell tonight, there must have been about fifty of us. Clive really looked after us, he'd be happy for the custom.

He'd organised some bingo – glad Mable and Gladys weren't there, it gave somebody else a chance to win. Clive's prices are cheaper than the club as well. But the downside is, in The Bell we have to buy our own drinks; in the club the men buy them for us.

Yes, it was a good night. There were dishes of free nuts and crisps at the bar. Free chip butties for 'after bird'. It was great.

Course, the gossip was all about the men.

We've decided to play them at their own game and have *Women Only* signs on our bedroom doors. Geraldine's going to get some professional-looking ones done.

"I think it's a *Please Enter* sign I need," I said.

Rose said she's read that we'll all be having sex in these virtual reality suits in the future. She can't wait, she said, she's trying to find out where she can put a deposit on one.

"Oh, great. Have they said how long we've got to wait for these virtual reality sex suits?" I said. "And will they do them in big sizes?"

"They said they would be on the market within the next ten to fifteen years. All sizes from an eight to a thirty-two."

"You had better get dieting then, Bev," Geraldine chuckled.

"You cheeky beggar. I am only a size twenty-four, thank you," I said, giving her a right dirty look. She knows I'm touchy about my weight.

"So will we be able to choose who we have a virtual with?" Geraldine said, changing the subject.

"Oh aye," Rose said. "You'll be able to choose which celebrity you have it with. The bigger the celeb, the bigger the price tags."

"I don't believe that," Geraldine said, looking gobsmacked. "Celebs telling everybody how big their penis is? I don't believe it."

We all looked at her – gone out, she is such a dope.

"Not size of their penis, size of their celebrity status. The bigger the star, the bigger the price."

"Oh, on second thoughts, you don't buy a banana unless you know how big it is, do you?"

"Shut up, Geraldine," I said. "Listen."

"So they'll be on a pay as you go, like your phones. Gerard Butler and Tom Cruise would be top of the range. We wouldn't be able to afford them."

"I'd remortgage my house to have a virtual with Gerard Butler," I said.

"Then would come your Sean Connerys, if you wanted a bit of old stuff. Might afford him if we saved up, or had him as a birthday pressie," Rose said.

"Oh yeah, I'm sure Baz would buy me a Sean Connery bonk for mi birthday," Geraldine joked.

"What if you're skint like me?" I said.

"I suppose if you're skint, we're talking Prince Charles, Malcolm Rifkind, Vladimir Putin. They'll be your cheapo types," Rose said.

"They'd have to pay *me* to have it with that lot," I said.

"Aye, but no virtual machine can ever reproduce the feeling of warm, naked flesh against your body," Cheryl said, smiling sensually, her eyelashes fluttering.

She would say that; her and Ralph have only been together for a couple of years, so they're still in the honeymoon period.

Then Geraldine piped up, "Or that feeling of a string vest coming down on you."

Well, we set off laughing and we could not stop. I nearly wet mi blooming knickers. I'm going to have to start carrying an extra pair around with me. We had a great night. Laugh? We nearly laughed our socks off.

Rose has got another date, Wayne. Hope it goes better than the others, she's very excited.

Got up because I couldn't sleep and I can hear Barry snoring from the other bedroom. Things are just going round and round in my head. I don't know what's happening to me and Barry. I'm a cow to him sometimes and then after I regret it. I was shattered when he moved into the other bedroom. He said at first it was because of him coughing, which he was, and I appreciated the gesture. But he's stayed there. I just don't think he loves me anymore. If he did he'd want to make love to me and he doesn't. He's only forty-five, for Christ's sake, he should be wanting it regular. Geraldine says her and Baz are at it nightly, and he's forty-seven. I still love him. I get so scared about the future and this problem at the club is not helping; it seems to be pushing us further apart.

I'll just have one more drink and then I might get some sleep.

BARRY

It was dead tonight in the club. We cancelled the bingo; there weren't enough punters in to bother. It's the women mainly that play the bingo; some of them are right experts, playing as many as six tickets a game. Mable and Gladys played hell and stormed out.

It's a good job they did, because a bloody big spider was let loose in the Men Only. When I say big, I mean big. Massive, it was – must have been about six to eight inches across. One of Charlie's pals had brought it in, in a Cunningham's Piccalilli jar, and the bloody thing escaped. It was scurrying all over the blooming room. Blokes were jumping up off their chairs, tables were getting knocked over – it was chaos.

I shouted, "Get that spider out of this club now or I'll tread on the bloody thing."

So there the dozy beggar is with his piccalilli jar, running around the room after the spider, shouting, "Andrea, come here, Andrea." Daft bat.

Amazingly he caught it and put it back in its jar. It was his pet apparently. How he didn't lose it I don't know.

Anyway, I chucked him and Andrea out.

I'm positive it was one of Charlie's schemes; he would have done it deliberately to get all the gossip going about gigantic spiders in the Men Only, hoping it would scare the women away. Crafty beggar he is, that Charlie.

I noticed that reporter was out front again; he looked in the piccalilli jar at Andrea. Then he scribbled something down in his notebook. I can't believe the news he gets from us is worth his while. Are there not more interesting things going on in the world?

BEV

Seems ever so strange, not going in the club. We have had to suspend our keep fit classes at The Blue Bell. It got full of men wanting to gawp at us doing our exercises, it was right off-putting. Hope I don't put weight on. They reckon the acts at the club have been fab. They have got to be better than the one we had last month; he was diabolical. He was a midget dressed up as a baby, he looked a right plonker. Everybody was booing him. So the concert secretary, Slimy Sam, went to pay him off, but he'd vanished, hadn't got a clue where he'd gone. Anyway, a young couple bonking round the back of the club heard these cries for help.

The silly sod had only jumped out of the dressing room window, landing in the rubbish bin, which was sited underneath the window. Not one of your ordinary household bins, but a massive oblong thing. I think he thought we'd be pelting things at him if he walked through the club. Well, he couldn't get out – he was tall for a midget, but he was still only about three foot two.

We all rushed outside to have a look what was going on. We like a bit of drama, brightens up the evening.

The midget was shouting, "For Christ's sake get me out. It stinks in here."

Well, I can imagine, it had been Pie and Peas Night a couple of days previous.

The committee men stood around the bin trying to peer inside, muttering to each other, trying to decide the best course of action, like men do. A couple of them were in charge of keeping us away. They love it when they can assert their authority over us mere boozers.

They decided that the best way to go about it was for a couple of them to lean in, each grab an arm and pull. But as they were pulling, he started screaming at the top of his voice.

"Let go, you're pulling my arms out of the bloody sockets."

Not wanting to make him armless they let go and he fell back into the bin, with a sickening slushing sound.

Then one of the lads, Shaun – he's a very tall, lanky lad – said, "Hold on to my legs and I'll lean in and grab him under the armpits, and when I shout, 'Pull', pull."

But before he could grab him, we heard this retching sound.

Then Shaun shouts, "Pull me back, I've puked up – the stink in here is vile, and my legs are bending the wrong way."

So they had to pull him back.

Baz shouted into the bin, "Don't worry, kid, we are working on it. We will have you out in no time. Hang on in there, help's coming."

At that point we sent Geraldine into the club to fetch our drinks.

"I'm covered in flaming puke now," the midget screamed.

Everybody was putting their spoke in, like they do.

Then the midget shouted, very angrily, "Are you going to get me out of this stinking garbage, you fucking morons?"

Everybody went silent – we were all gobsmacked. Language like that coming from a midget in a Babygro. Disgusting. We didn't expect that!

Baz leaned the top of his head into the bin and shouted, "Hey, mate, don't go shouting at us, it's your own bloody fault you're in there."

"I didn't leave the fucking bin lid open," he shouts. You could tell he was getting a bit frustrated.

Then old Charlie pipes up, "Leave him in there, the ungrateful bastard. He should get some better jokes. Silly sod."

I think the midget then realised it was not a good idea to antagonise his rescuers, so he apologised and said he was a bit stressed out.

Then Ralph came up with a right good idea. He suggested that the midget lean against the side of the bin and the men slowly bring it on to its side, so he could crawl out. Everybody agreed it was a great idea.

Well, he emerged from that bin screaming his head off. All the slush from the bottom of the bin had slid as they turned it on its side. He whooshed out. Mushy peas can be very slippery. It reminded me of an elephant giving birth, not that I've ever seen one.

He was covered. Greens, browns, yellows – every colour you could think of. He could have stood in Hyde Park as a piece of modern art, and he probably would have won the Turner Prize. Like that woman with the dirty bed covered in sperm and used condoms.

You would have thought that little midget was an alien. You couldn't recognise him as a human being. Folk were retching right, left and centre. But we all gave a sigh of relief. The main thing was, he was out.

He limped slowly back to the club entrance. The steward wouldn't let him inside. They offered to hose him down, which he accepted. Stupid Dennis turned the hose on too hard and as the stream of water hit him, he was pushed up off his feet and landed face down on the tarmac. Definitely not his day.

We were all thinking what more could happen to this poor little man. His nose was a bit bruised but other than that he looked alright. Geraldine pointed out that one of his arms did look longer than the other. We said it must be out of its socket. It certainly was a 'bless him' moment.

He looked like death and I bet he thought he was going to die in that bin; it must have looked massive to someone his size.

Because the bins are round the back, we wouldn't have seen or heard anything as we left the club. Rowdy lot, us, when we've had a drink. It could have been a disastrous death for him if that couple hadn't been bonking.

They got him a large brandy. The steward knocked him 10% off. He asked Barry to ring his wife to fetch him; he said he was too shocked to drive. Before him and his wife left, credit due, he apologised. The concert sec told him to ditch the Babygro, get some better jokes and he would give him another booking.

We all waved them off. He didn't ask for his fee. I know we shouldn't have, but after it had all settled down we couldn't stop laughing. Best night we've had in ages.

So the poor unlucky sod was worth the money he didn't get after all.

BARRY

I found a birthday card behind the bread bin. It said on the front, *To my husband*. She'd written nothing inside. Oh well.

I rang Marks and Sparks. They liked me and I have gone on a list of possible future employees. Great! And they'll be in touch if another position comes up. That's hopeful.

BEV

Geraldine popped in for a cup of tea today. She was dead miserable. She plonked herself down on a kitchen chair; then she gave a sigh. She obviously wanted me to notice how depressed she was feeling.

"So," I said, very sympathetically, "what's up with you?" She looked like she'd just learned she'd got cancer or some other terminal condition.

She gave another sigh. Her eyes were saying, *Come on, ask me again.*

So I did.

"Come on, Geraldine, love," I said. "Tell me, what's up?" She looked at me; then sighed again.

I was getting a little bit fed up now. I think she realised I was about to change the subject.

"Oh, it's…" She paused; then sighed *again*.

"Yes?" I shouted, nodding my head six to the dozen.

"Well, it's…since I chucked Baz into the other bedroom…I'm missing my daily dose of sex."

I relaxed and blew air from my lungs.

She sat there, her head down on one side and her doleful eyes looking up at me.

"Well, I don't know what you're expecting me to do about *that*, Geraldine," I said, "but whatever it is I am not going to do it."

I thought something really serious had happened and it was just that she is not getting her daily dose of sex. *Pathetic or what?* I thought.

Daily dose? She should be so lucky – we haven't had sex for months.

We once went on a caravan holiday with her and Baz, and every night the caravan would bounce up and down. They seemed to be at it all night. It was a nightmare for me and Barry.

Next morning they were all smiles, while me and Barry were tired out and suffering from a kind of seasickness that had been inflicted on us by the rocking caravan. Then they would go to bed in the afternoon and sleep for about five hours.

"Never again," Barry said.

I gave her a cuppa. Then she starts telling me about this fetish she's got for men in stonewashed jeans with creases. Apparently the crotch area drives her crackers. *She's blooming daft*, I thought.

"What about bleach-washed jeans?" I asked her. I was being sarcastic, but she didn't notice.

"No, doesn't do anything for me. They have to be stonewashed."

It goes back to when she saw The Hollies live in concert. She was sat on the front row looking up at them and they were all wearing stonewashed jeans with creases.

I told her about my fetish for men in Cuban heels, although I think it's now police inspectors with white hair and in uniform.

She says she has this recurring sexual fantasy that she's the only woman left in the world, and all the rest of us have died of some disease that only women can get.

Great, I thought.

She's on a cruise ship, naked, with a crew of rampant men like the ones in *South Pacific* singing *There is Nothing*

Like a Dame. They're all in stonewashed jeans with creases. She is dramatic. She's desperate for some nooky by the sounds of it.

I told her, "It's not natural at your age. You're a bloody nymphomaniac. You should go to the doctors."

"I am a nymphomaniac," she said proudly. "I was diagnosed by a doctor when I was twenty-six. It is an accepted medical condition."

"The doctor, how did that come about?" I was dead curious.

"It was Baz – he was physically going downhill and they did all sorts of tests on him but they couldn't find anything wrong. It turned out it was exhaustion, too much sex. It was doing him in. Doctors said if we didn't slow down he wouldn't last till he was thirty."

"How old was he?" I quizzed.

"Twenty-nine. So we had to make a lifesaving decision and cut it down to once a day."

"Oh right?" I nodded. I decided I needed a biscuit.

Then she went on to tell me she thinks Father Pickles fancies her.

"Fancies you? Don't be daft! He's a blooming Catholic priest!" I nearly choked on my biscuit.

Geraldine is one of them women that thinks that every man fancies her.

"He talks and talks to me, I have trouble getting away from him," she said. "He tells me all sorts of rubbish, and I know it's just to keep me there after the other women have left."

"He talks rubbish anyway," I said.

"I know that, but he's talking it for longer. He fancies me, I know he does."

I couldn't get my breath. "He's a Catholic priest, Geraldine," I said again. "They are supposed to be celibate."

"You believe that, do you?" she said sarcastically.

"No, I suppose not."

"Least he hasn't got a wife to make things complicated." She smiled.

I thought, *She's going to do it.*

She said that since that incident at the church, when Baz told him to shove the bishop up his effing cassock, he's started calling at their house for a cup of tea. And there's loads of innuendo in his chat.

"Like what?" I asked.

"Well, like, he asks me about my fantasies on the cruise ship with all the men."

"That's not innuendo. That's blatant. Anyhow, how does he know about the cruise ship and all the men?" I was intrigued.

"I told him," she said.

"What?! You told him? Why?"

"In confession."

She's mad, I thought.

Then the phone rang – it was our Julie. Was I glad. I said I'd see Geraldine later, and she left.

I've never been unfaithful to Barry. Well, there was that time on the ladies' section weekend trip to Blackpool. I got a bit sozzled and snogged a bloke from Cleckheaton. I felt really guilty about that. But I've never been properly unfaithful to him. I just wouldn't. No, I *couldn't*. Even though I've got my suspicions about him.

BARRY

There was a right performance at the club today.

Mable and Gladys were on their scooters coming into the car park and Albert and Charlie were on theirs leaving the car park, and what did Mable and Albert do? They crashed into each other. Well, it started a bloody riot between them.

Mable said Albert was driving too fast, which I know he does. He drives around the car park like it's blooming Brands Hatch.

Albert said Mable weren't looking where she was going. I know that's true as well. She's nearly knocked me over a couple of times. Her and Gladys drive along two abreast, chatting away to each other, never looking where they are going.

He called her a blind old biddy.

She called him a mad old twit.

Albert said Mable was a menace and should be banned from driving.

Then Charlie put his spoke in and said, "This is a working men's club and the women shouldn't be allowed to park."

Gladys put her spoke in and said that Charlie doesn't work.

All four of them were shouting at each other.

"You want barring."

"You want barring, you mean."

"No, you want barring."

"No, *you* want barring."

They like a bunch of kids. They say when you get older you go backwards, and they certainly have.

So I barred all four of them for the rest of the day. You could hear them shouting abuse at each other all the way down Main Street.

The women are still going into The Bell. No communication between us. The club's not doing too well in the week; we had to cancel bingo again.

I took a cut-up apple to my squirrel pal today; he wolfed it down. Then he looked at me – I'm sure he was asking for more. When he realised I hadn't got any more, he just ran off.

BEV

Got on the scales today – put on two pounds. I was fuming. I don't know how the bloody hell that's happened. I've tried.

Okay, I've fell down some times. The baby food diet obviously didn't work. Mind you, I did eat all twenty-four jars in four days. *I've got to do something*, I thought. So I went for a walk, and I hadn't gone far before I went all dizzy – must have been my sugar levels dropping. Lucky I was near the paper shop, so I bought a couple of Mars bars, and felt a lot better after eating them.

I walked right up to Sainsbury's and back, must be about two miles. In calories, about two or three hundred, I think.

I felt good knowing I'm doing something about it.

I went on the internet and ordered a pedometer and a vibrating machine. They say you just stand on it and it vibrates all your fat away. I hope so.

Rose's date with Wayne went well, she says he's lovely.

I said, "Are his fingernails clean and is he married?"

She said yes to the first and no to the second question. She is very excited.

Cheryl called; she was upset. I think I must be the blooming local agony aunt because everybody comes to me with their problems, as though I haven't got enough of my own. Still, they are my mates and that's what mates are for.

It was their first anniversary of living together yesterday – gosh, how time flies. Anyway, Ralph had fetched them an Indian. They'd opened a bottle of champagne and they were going to have a right romantic evening. He'd even sprinkled their pillows with rose petals, she said. They were going to have a night of sexual ecstasy. They were just on their onion bhaji starter when the phone rang – it was his son, Denver. He had to hand his history project in at school the next day and his computer had broken down or whatever computers do. It was his last day and it was an exam paper. He wanted his dad to have a look at his computer. Apparently Ralph's a bit of a wizard with computers. So he went; said he wouldn't be long.

At ten past ten Cheryl went to bed. Not before binning all the food, emptying the champagne down the sink, flushing the rose petals down the loo, and bolting the bedroom door. When she got up this morning he'd already gone to work. She hasn't seen him since. They love each other like mad; you only have to look at them to see it. But these problems with his ex-wife and son are driving her crackers. Something will have to happen or I doubt they will survive.

BARRY

Guess what? We have a big sign stuck to the kitchen cupboard door: *FOOD WILL KILL*. And there's a picture of a hearse with four bearers, and one of them looks like me. I don't know who's supposed to be in the coffin.

Looked for the butter; it's gone again. And the packet of bacon I was fancying for my dinner – that's gone as well.

Fridge is full of salads, fruit and healthy yoghurts. It will all go to rot and then be thrown into the bin. The dustbin is full of stuff that was in the fridge yesterday. It's happened before, hundreds of times. She's a wasteful beggar. It's a bloody vicious circle with her.

When I mentioned Weight Watchers, she said she doesn't want folk knowing how much she weighs. I mean, you only have to look at her. It's not something she can disguise. I wish she would either get some help or accept the fact that that is the way she is and stop all this bloody yo-yo stuff. Oh well, it's up to her in the end.

Saturday concerts are still doing well, got some good acts lined up for next month.

BEV

Bought a gorgeous top today, and it's a size too small for me. My aim is to slim myself into it and then buy another, a size smaller than that, and so on and on. I've hung it in the kitchen near the fridge door where I can see it, so when I feel like eating I see it and don't. Hope it will give me some incentive. Barry left £20 on the kitchen counter to pay for it.

It's very strange – I've noticed it before, but he doesn't look as ugly to me today because of his generosity. When I really hate him, he looks dead ugly. That mole on his chin looks massive and it seems to send vibrations out towards me. But when he's generous like today, I hardly notice it. Must be something to do with sex hormones.

I've cut a photo of a model out of a magazine, cut the head off and stuck a picture of my head on it. I wanted to see what I would look like slim. I look absolutely fabulous. I'm dead chuffed with myself. I've stuck it on the fridge door so every time I am tempted to go in the fridge I see the photo and drool over myself. Will the new top and photo work their magic on me? I hope so.

There was some reporters came in The Bell tonight. They started pestering us; they are dead persistent. We told them to get lost, but they wouldn't. Clive had to throw them out in the end. So far there is nothing to tell them anyway, it's stalemate. Bloody stalemate. We're not talking to the men about it and they're not talking to us about it. It's as though the problem doesn't exist. We go in The Bell and they go in the club. Clive the landlord says we can have a line dancing night and of course we are having our bingo. How long this will go on for is anybody's guess.

Rose is seeing Wayne again. She can't wait – I wonder if this is the soulmate she's looking for? She's bought a new bra, so it must be serious.

BARRY

I had to go to the chippy for my dinner. There's no decent food in the house. Rose served me, and there was less chips this time. She slung them on the counter. She didn't give me any eye contact. I'm going to have to change my chippy.

Next week Bev will have got fed up again, and the lettuce, fruit, salads and yoghurts will be in the dustbin and the cupboards will be full of the sort of stuff that was in the dustbin last week.

Lads at the club were talking about computer games. They seem to all play them, or the younger ones anyway. I felt left out, so I went to Game and I've bought myself one, it's called *Call of Duty*. It's good; I'm right into it. Not a very good shot though, but I'm practising.

I'm fed up of seeing the women's leaflets stuck all over the blooming place – bus stops, street lights. Albert said they even have one in the doctor's waiting room. There was one stuck on the farmer's gate leading to the woods. The women are certainly going for it.

BEV

My pedometer and my vibrating machine arrived today.

It took ages to put the vibrator together. I rang Rose and she came to help me before she went to work.

She told me she thinks it's the real thing with this Wayne fella. She's thinking about him all the time and he rang her four times yesterday, for no reason, just to talk. One call was one hour and seven minutes. And she let him fondle her breasts under her jumper but over her new bra. She's got it bad. She says she's buying all new underwear and she's going to have her pubic hair shaped like a heart before she goes all the way.

It's a right big thing, this vibrator machine. I got on it and it shook me to bits. I had to get off. I thought, *I'm going to get shaken brain syndrome*. I was a bit disappointed so I put my pedometer on and went for a walk.

I made the mistake of walking past the chippy. The smell – it was like having an orgasm. I couldn't resist; I went in and bought chips, fish and mushy peas, and a battered sausage for afters. Rose served me; she was going on about the fabulous Wayne again.

I sat on the wall to eat my fish and chips. Well, I couldn't eat them looking at my new top hung on the kitchen door. The good news is I did 1,631 steps. So I'm doing something.

I think I am going to go on the cabbage diet. You poo a lot but it works, apparently.

I stuck a few leaflets up while I was walking. We have got to keep focused.

BARRY

One of the women has stuck a blooming poster on the war memorial – can you believe it? I ripped it off; what are they thinking of?

Oh, there's a space, I think I'll stick a poster on it.

Went for a walk today, but I didn't go my usual route, the route I've been going for the last few years. So I didn't see my pal the squirrel.

It's funny how you get stuck in a routine. I went down to the Jones' farm, across the field, and then up into the woods.

This time I went straight down what we as youngsters used to call Lovers' Lane. Don't know its real name. I don't think it has one. It brings you out on the other side of the woods. There I came across something I'd forgotten long ago. A carving I'd done on a tree: a heart with *Barry loves Bev*. I couldn't believe it; it was still there. I remember doing it years ago. We'd gone for a walk and it had started raining, so we sheltered under this tree and I carved it.

It's like it was yesterday. I stood looking at it for ages. It made me think about that first time I went out with Bev.

She was a beautiful girl, slim, long blonde hair. All the lads wanted to take her out. I didn't ask her for ages; I thought she wouldn't want to go out with me. I was right surprised when I did ask her out that she said yes. We went to the pictures – I thought if I got tongue-tied we'd just watch the film and that would be that. But I didn't, we just talked and talked. We got on great. Asked her out again and before we knew it we were a couple. We were crazy about each other.

A year later we were married, and six months after that we had our first baby. We called her Rachael; she came prematurely. It was a difficult birth for Bev and bless the little soul, she died, aged nine hours. Course we were devastated.

Bev wanted to get pregnant again straight away, and we did, which I thought was brave of Bev seeing as she'd had such a bad time.

Our Julie was born thirteen months later. We were happy, really happy.

Oh God, what the bloody hell's happened to us? Where is all that happiness we once felt?

BEV

Off the cabbage diet, it's rubbish. It's just cabbage. Got a booklet on it and everything is cabbage.

Tried the vibrating machine again, only managed two minutes. My thighs were wobbling like jelly. I'm sure it must do me some good, if I could just stick at it. But it wobbles my brain as well. It scares me. I don't want to end up like Muhammad Ali, bless him.

Geraldine came round for a cuppa. I couldn't believe it. She's having an affair with Father Pickles. Or Peter, as she now calls him. She said she knew all along he fancied her.

"Do you think he'd like a threesome?" I was being sarcastic, and she ignored me.

"He is absolutely fantastic in bed," she said.

"Oh good, I'm glad for you," I answered.

Her and Baz have never done anything like what her and Peter are doing. She said they have matching black leather G-strings.

"Oh my God, you don't?" I nearly dropped my biscuit.

"We do, and nipple clamps. Red, they are."

"Red nipple clamps? Do they hurt?" I said, swallowing my biscuit.

"I don't wear them, they're for him, and pink tickly condoms."

"Geraldine, what are you doing? And what do you want pink tickly condoms for? You're on the pill," I said, picking up another biscuit.

"It's not to do with birth control, it's the playful pleasure you get from them." She was getting right excited as she talked about what they get up to. Some of it sounded physically impossible, but they are both very slim so I suppose that makes a difference. I have trouble getting my socks on.

Then the phone went – it was our Julie. As I was busy chatting to our Julie, I glanced back at Geraldine; she looked very strange. Her eyes were glazed over and her breathing was really laboured. I told our Julie I would talk later.

I thought, *Golly, whatever's up with her?* Then I realised what it was; I get it myself. It was her sugar levels, they were dropping. You can go into a coma if they drop too low.

So I poured her another cup of tea and put three sugars in; then I got her a Mars bar. It took her a while but she came round. She drank her tea, but she didn't want the Mars bar.

Geraldine is one of my best friends but I was actually glad when she'd gone. I can't believe what she is doing. Still, it's her life. He was right, that doctor, though: she is a blooming nympho.

I just couldn't get mi mind around what she'd told me. I'd got this picture in my head of Father Pickles going into a sex shop in his cassock and asking for some tickly pink condoms, nipple clamps and a pair of matching black leather G-strings. It's like a sketch from Benny Hill.

An image of a suitcase of money flashed before my eyes. I bet I could get thousands from the Sunday papers for this. It would be in the headlines: *THE SEXY PRIEST AND THE TICKLY PINK CONDOMS*.

I had a cup of sweet tea and ate the Mars bar. Then I got a text from Geraldine; it just said, *Sorry, forgot to take the egg out, LOL Geraldine.*

She's daft, she's barmy, a nympho as well
That sex-crazed priest got her under his spell
Tickly pink condoms and red nipple clamps
The positions they get in would give me the cramps

I'm gobsmacked and shocked that she'd even dare
Have an orgasm sat on my kitchen chair
I thought she was having a low sugar bout
I shoved her a Mars bar before she passed out

If Baz finds out, there'll be trouble, oh yes
Peter Pickles, beware: with Baz you don't mess
He'll give you a beating; then to you he'll confess
You'll have to forgive him – well, more or less

I'm so glad I am faithful to Barry, although
I've had the odd thought of some rich gigolo
But I never would do it, I'm just not that sort
Anyway, with my luck I'm sure I'd get caught

I love him to pieces, my Barry, I do
I'll love him forever and I know that is true
But we've grown far apart, it's so sad, it's a shame
And I certainly know that I'm partly to blame

If we could just talk, figure it out
What is it that's driving us so far apart?
I hope to God that it's not too late
My Barry, my love, please come back, my soulmate

BARRY

They came to empty the fruit machines today. We usually get over a hundred quid commission, but it was less than fifty.

Just shows who uses the machines more: the women.

I went a long walk in the woods. I didn't see my squirrel pal. I looked for him; don't know where he was. I'd taken some apple, so I left it by the tree he usually runs up. Hope he got it.

It's so peaceful down there. Kids don't seem to play in the woods anymore like we did. I suppose their parents are frightened of letting them out of their sight these days.

Cowboys and Indians – I always liked being an Indian,

you got to wear the feathers and I wasn't bad with the old bow and arrow.

Then we played at war. We'd get our water pistols and at the end, the wettest of us were the losers. Our mothers weren't too pleased if we lost.

I suppose the kids of today are playing the same games but on their computers. It's a shame. I know which is the healthiest.

When I got back to the club that reporter was there, hovering round the club again. I told him in no uncertain terms to bugger off and not come back; there was nothing here for him. He just shrugged his shoulders; then left. It's making me bloody mad, him being there all the time. Hope he stays away now.

BEV

Barry's been off on one of his walking jaunts today. One of these days I'm going to follow him, see what he gets up to. If he's seeing somebody else…Well, I don't know what I would do.

It would be an understatement to say we're not getting on of late. Him in one bedroom; me in the other. He reckons it's because the bed's too small. It's a king-size, how much blinking room does he need? It's not as though he's going to jump off the top of the wardrobe in an eyepatch and a black leather glove.

Perhaps I should take a leaf out of Geraldine's book and

have an affair. Well, you only live once, as they say. It's not a rehearsal. I reckon Freddy the window cleaner fancies me a bit. He looks at me all funny like, when I give him his four quid. A bit poppy, they are, his eyes. He's a pleasant enough bloke, but he's no Gerard Butler. He's got pock marks, and sometimes he has snot dripping from his nose – well, I exaggerate there; once, last winter, and it wasn't dripping because it was frozen. At first I thought it must be a new fashion because it looked like a diamond hanging down from his left nostril. I mean, nothing would surprise me these days. They have stuff all over their bodies. But when I put my glasses on to see into my purse, I could see it was frozen snot. It looked a bit like an opal. I gave him a tissue, and he snapped it off.

I wonder if he's one of them blokes that like fat women; I've seen a programme about them on the telly. They're called 'feeders', and they like to feed the women up, make them even fatter, so they are totally dependent and other men don't fancy them.

There was one American woman, thirty-seven stone, never moved off the bed. Her husband had to wash her, feed her, do everything for her. Got to be his fault she was like she was, because he went shopping for the food.

I've always wondered, though, how they manage to have sex. I mean, how would you find it amongst all those layers?

Anyway, this woman had a stomach bypass. She lost twenty-three stone and her husband divorced her. Weird.

I've been thinking about getting a vibrator, but I'd be worried that Barry would hear it whirring in the next bedroom. I like him to think it's not bothering me. Sex, me? Not interested. Lying cow, I am.

I'll just have to stick to mi own devices for the time being.

I'm getting like blooming Geraldine, obsessed with sex. I'm going to have to stop reading them novels. Still, it's probably that I'm not getting it, that's the problem.

Rose came round; she was devastated. Wayne had come into the chip shop and seen her.

I said, "So?"

She said, "I'd told him I was a PA for a director of a big firm called Robbis."

"Robbis?" I said, totally confused. "But you've worked at the chippy for six years."

"I made it up," she said. "Anyway, he came in and I even served him. He wanted two fishcakes, large chips and mushy peas. I love him," she cried, tears rolling down her face.

"So what did he do?" I asked, passing her the kitchen roll.

"Well, I did them for him and I gave him loads of chips, but I was so embarrassed I forgot to ask him if he wanted salt and vinegar. He took them and left, then when he got outside he pressed his face against the window and just stared at me, shook his head and walked off.

"Oh dear." It was all I could think of to say.

"And then after he'd gone, the boss said, 'You forgot to offer that man salt and vinegar, Rose. It's not a sacking offence but the company take a dim view of that sort of behaviour and it will go down on your employment record.'"

I said to her, "Why did you tell Wayne you were a PA?"

"It just sounded better than 'chip shop serving person'. I told him on our first date, before I fell for him. That's what everybody does on the dating sites: tell lies to make themselves sound more interesting. Oh bloody, bloody, bloody hell. I bet he hates me now."

She was near hysteria.

"What was he doing in the chip shop anyway?" I asked her.

"He was getting something to eat." She looked at me as though I was daft.

"I know that," I said. "I mean—"

"Well, he text me after and said he was in the neighbourhood but he didn't expect to see me serving in a chip shop. Then another text said, GOODBYE, LYING WOMAN, and it was in…capitals."

I put my arm around her. "Does he not know it's only clean people that can work in chip shops?" I said. It was the only thing I could think of. I made her a coffee and she calmed down a bit. I changed the subject. I told her that we hadn't had any dog crap on the garden for ages. She didn't seem very interested. Then she just up and left, taking my kitchen roll with her. I wasn't bothered; I've got another two-pack.

Then I thought about what my dad always used to say: he would sooner have a thief than a liar.

BARRY

Cheryl is doing an interview on tonight's local TV news programme. I don't know whether I will watch it. I'm fed up of it all now. It's got way out of control. Both sides are entrenched. They are like a set of kids. It's become a normal way of life now: women in The Bell, men in the club. A simple compromise at the beginning from the men, like the women going into the Men Only on a Saturday night, would have saved all this bloody bother. But we are past that now.

I doubt the women will back down on the full membership issue. If they don't get it, I reckon it's ten to one the club will be closed within a year.

I feel like putting the lot of them, men and women, in a bag and shaking them up and saying, "Do you know what you are doing, all of you?"

The club has always been the centre of everything that goes on in the village. I was a youngster in 1984 when the miners' strike was on. All their meetings were held in the club. It also acted as a soup kitchen for them that were struggling with big families. Losing the club would be such a loss to the village. A big, big loss.

Saw my pal the squirrel again. Would it be too daft to think that he looks for me? He came right up close. He was only about a couple of feet away from me. I tried to touch him but he moved back, then he edged his way towards me again. I got his apple out and placed it on the floor. He stood a bit; then he grabbed at it and ran off. Brilliant, bloody brilliant.

BEV

Cheryl has been interviewed on *BBC Look North*, the news programme. They came to the house with all their cameras and sound things. She asked me to go over because she was a bit nervous. All the neighbours were outside watching. They must have been wondering what was going on.

She was very good, I'm glad it weren't me. She was so articulate. She said that the men are fighting a losing battle and they know it. That the club cannot survive without the women – we put our money over the bar just like the men. And that we contribute in other ways too.

Like when there's a darts march and there's a visiting team. Who makes all the sandwiches, hands them out? The women.

Football section. Who washes all their mucky, smelly gear? The women. Well, Karen in particular; she gets paid for it, £1.50 per kit. Who cheers them on whether they are winning or losing? The women.

She told them about the Easter bonnet competition, a tradition going back years, and what a great day it is. All the family get involved: mothers, dads, grandmothers, granddads, everybody. The atmosphere is great, kids enjoying the magicians and jugglers. There's sandwiches, pie and peas, pizzas, all made and supplied by the women. A fantastic day; a tradition that goes back years.

She said she didn't think the men would make and wear the bonnets. She mentioned the miners' strike. How the women of that time had run a soup kitchen, and how they had raised money to help the miners with families to buy the kids shoes and school uniforms.

She said, "That was one of the bad times, but the women stood beside the men, all together."

And when Dennis' wife was dying of cancer, how the women took it in turns to take her to the hospital for her radiotherapy and sat with her when she was dying while Dennis went to work.

Yes, and we didn't just sit with her when he was working – we sat with her when he went boozing as well, I thought.

She said, "The men have actually gutted us with their decision. But we are not going to give in. We are worth more than that."

She made me cry. I'd got tears streaming down my face.

I could see tears in her eyes as well. She was so fab. I hope that when it goes out, all those truths will hit the men hard. She had integrity by the bucketful.

It's not just about sitting in the Men Only now, or getting full membership – it's about the men's attitude towards the women.

BARRY

I did watch Cheryl's television interview. It was good; hope some of the men listened to it.

It's getting personal now. There's been an article in the local freebie newspaper; it said, *Unemployed secretary of the Kenthorpe Miners' Welfare Club, Barry Allsop, and his wife Bev, who works at the local petrol station, are at the opposite ends and forefront of the warring factions*.

'Unemployed secretary' makes me sound like a scrubber who lives off my wife. I've never lived off a woman yet, and I've no intention of doing so. I'd kill my bloody self before I'd do that.

I don't know who said it. I bet it's one of the women. I hope to God it wasn't Bev.

Them two old sods Albert and Charlie are beginning to get on my tits now. They go on and on about the women, calling them all sorts of names.

I said to them, "Stop it, you're talking about our wives, and if you don't want to end up with a thick ear, *shut it*."

BEV

Barry's really mad about the local freebie interview. I daren't tell him it was me they interviewed – well, not really an interview, more a slanging match in the street. I must have said things I don't remember saying.

But I do know for a fact that I never said that Barry was unemployed. They must have gone fishing elsewhere. I've made my mind up; I'm not doing any more slanging matches in the streets. I am going to have to learn to turn a blind eye. I could tell it had upset Barry – he didn't eat his dinner.

I saw Father Peter Pickles in Marks and Spencer's today – well, I saw him trip over an old woman's walking frame. Four assistants came fussing around him, asking if he was alright. I must say he's a very attractive and charming man, I can see why Geraldine fancies him, and in his cassock the women love him. I expect they feel safe. If only they knew. I felt like shouting out, "Do you know he wears a black leather thong, nipple clamps and a tickly pink condom?"

He was buying some stonewash jeans, can you believe?

He spoke to me, in his polite, posh voice. (Funny how

all the clergy seem to talk posh and quiet. You never hear them saying, "Eyup, mi cocker" or "How tha doing, pal?")

"Hello, Beverly," he said. "Just buying myself a pair of jeans."

"Stonewash?" I said.

"Yes, very good guess, I like the stonewash." He was smiling with all his face. I bet he was imagining Geraldine pulling his zipper down.

I thought, *Yes, I know what you are going to be getting up to in them, you little pervert.* I just haven't got the respect for him now. Every time I see him I think about him in his black G-string and his nipple clamps. Oh, he makes mi sugar levels drop.

I had to buy a bar of chocolate.

BARRY

A letter came this morning addressed to the committee. It's special, this one. I read it out loud to the committee. It said:

Dear brothers in arms,

I write in support of your admirable and necessary stand. I urge you not to give in, for to do so would be the thin end of a rotten, maggot-ridden wedge.

If these haggish harridans were to get their grasping talons on your committee, their mischievous malevolence would spread like the Black Death.

Make no mistake: for all their fluttering of eyelashes and their simpering ways, they are serpents with souls of poison.

If you want to stay out of the insane asylum, then maintain the sanctuary that is your committee room.

Be brave of heart, for all our sakes, and we will win through.

Yours,
James Ratonbury, Colonel (retired)

The address was Borndean Psychiatric Hospital. I bet his room is nice and padded.

Actually, I showed it to our lass and for the first time in ages we had a good laugh together.

It saddens me that me and Bev are where we are. I just don't know how to get us back to where we were. This situation is not helping. We have always had a good marriage. I know getting a job would help. She works and she resents me for not working. I'm trying, I really am trying, I'm going for the most menial of jobs and I can't even get them.

There has been such a lot of trauma in our lives over the last couple of years. First her brother Phil got killed on his motorbike. That was a right shock to all of us. She was very close to him. He was a good lad, I got on with him. What was also upsetting was that within two month his wife was living with another bloke. Must have been going on before he got killed, that little liaison. Bev didn't half give her what for. Then a couple of months after that her mother died of a heart attack. I think Phil's death and all the trouble that surrounded it had a lot to do with that, she was never right after he died. Anybody who has kids understands that.

Then me losing my job. My God, when I think about it we haven't half had some bad luck.

And I know how she struggles with her weight. Since her mother and their Phil died she's put on quite a few stone. She eats, she can't seem to help it; she just eats.

When I do the shopping I don't bring any cakes or biscuits that's fattening. But what does she do – she brings them from the garage, and I bet she's gorging when she working as well. Only time will tell.

We got quite a few letters from men, some of them saying that they let their women on their committee and it was a big mistake. They have taken over, they say, and marriages have suffered. That's what I'm worried about here.

Some letters called us male chauvinists. Everybody has their own opinion.

BEV

Right performance this morning. I was in my bedroom stark naked, I'd had my shower. I'm stood in front of the full-length mirror, looking at my body. What a sight.

I'd heard the lasses talking about trimming their pubic hair. *Mine is a bit bushy*, I thought. So I got my scissors and I was halfway through trimming them when I heard this singing.

"I'm a rhinestone cowboy…" It was Freddy the window

cleaner; he'd popped up to clean my bedroom window. Our house is elevated from the road. You can't even see in my bedroom from the top of the double-decker buses that pass, so I don't bother closing the blinds. Well, I just froze. Then instinct took over and I dived on to the floor. I lay there on the carpet, naked, for about five minutes, or so it seemed. My back was itching like mad, it's right fluffy, my bedroom carpet.

He washes all the frames and sills every three months. I thought, *I bet it's today*, and it was. I sneaked a look over the top of my bed. And he'd gone, so I struggled up and then he appeared again; he'd have to move his ladder because it's a bay window. I dived back down. I just lay there like four pence. I daren't move, and I think I must have fallen asleep because when I looked through the window he was doing Mrs Brown's windows, halfway down the street.

I don't know what he saw. I know he saw something because when he came for his money later there was a distinct funny look on his face that I thought said, *Ha ha, I have seen you naked*.

My back has been itching where I can't reach it all day. I'd ask Barry to scratch it for me but he might think I'm coming on to him, so I thought better of it.

Went in The Bell tonight with the lasses, and Clive handed us this bag full of letters. Well, we had a right laugh reading them.

One woman said that they haven't got a Men Only but they have got a stupid roped-off area where the men can take their dogs and ferrets, but not their wives.

She said since they saw Cheryl on the telly, the women got out their scissors and cut the rope.

So keep up the good work, we are in full support.
The Ollershaw Ladies' Section, Brighouse

One bloke said he heard me on the radio and he thought I sounded very sexy, and would I sit on him?

Geraldine said, "He wouldn't be asking that if he'd seen you on the television instead."

She is a cheeky beggar; she never puts her brain into gear before she speaks. I glared at her. She quickly realised what she'd said and apologised, and then she offered to get a round in.

Cheryl had one fella that asked for a pair of her panties. She said she is going to send them a pair of Ralph's underpants before she washes them.

Most of the letters were supporting us; it made us feel good and want to carry on with our quest, for want of a better word.

We had a great night, though, had a right laugh. We're beginning to settle in The Bell; only thing is, it's costly having to buy our own drinks.

BARRY

Went upstairs this morning, and Bev's bedroom door was wide open and there she was fast asleep, laid out stark naked on the bedroom floor. I couldn't believe my eyes. I stood for a minute having a look. Then I thought, *Now could this be the ideal time to test myself.* I was hoping I might get some stirrings downstairs in my penis. I moved closer, looking, taking it all in. I thought when I was younger I couldn't get enough of Bev's body. We were like rabbits. Every chance we got we were at it.

But I was getting nothing, not even a twitch. What the fuck is happening to us, or me, should I say? Have we gone stale? Don't I fancy her anymore? I love her; I know that, so why can't I get an erection? Is it me? I don't know. Is my sex life over at forty-five? I bloody hope not.

Mind you, in my defence it wasn't the ideal situation: she was snoring away with her mouth wide open, slaver running down her cheek on to the carpet. Her breasts had fallen to the sides and she looked like she'd had a bad haircut in the nether region. Not really a sexually arousing sight.

Bev needs to cut down on her booze, and she needs to get off some of that weight. I love her, though.

I finally got the vote I've canvassed for, to hopefully save the club. Seven to five – close, but we've done it. The women can go in the Men Only, but only on a Saturday night.

I've just got to persuade the women now. Hopefully they'll understand that the main aim should be for all of us to get the club back on its feet financially. Then we can discuss this other demand, full membership for the women. I just can't imagine Kenthorpe without the club. It's the hub of the community.

Our troubles should have been halfway over. Then Dennis came rushing into the office.

"You'd better get to the Men Only. They've barricaded themselves in," he said, eyes bulging.

I couldn't believe it. I got to the Men Only door, pushed at it, but it wouldn't budge.

"Open this bloody door," I shouted, banging the door with my fist.

"We don't want women in here. This room is for men only and we plan to keep it that way." I recognised Albert's voice.

"It's a committee decision and anybody that doesn't abide by it could be barred," I shouted back. I was getting angry now; I thought we'd practically solved it and now this.

Dennis, who had followed me from the office, whispered, "You can't bar Albert and Charlie, they're life members. Albert was the president for twenty years, you can't bar him."

I said, "It's Albert bloody Robson, he was president of the Kenthorpe Miners' Club. He's not bloody Barack Obama."

"Go and fetch us some fish and chips, Dennis." That was Charlie's voice shouting.

"I want vinegar on mine. And we might need some sleeping bags later," shouts Albert.

"Stop being daft bats and open this bloody door." I banged hard on the door; folks were coming out of the other rooms to see what was going on.

"Over our dead bodies," came the reply.

They're not going to open this door, I thought.

So what I did was go through the games room, into part of the steward's quarters and out into the Men Only, through the bar. Dennis and Baz and a few of the other blokes followed me.

When we got into the Men Only they didn't see us as they were facing the door. We were stood behind them. They'd barricaded the door with piled-up tables and chairs.

"It's gone very quiet out there," Albert said.

"It's because they know who they are dealing with. We're not pushovers," Charlie said.

"I'm hoping it's because they've gone to get us the fish and chips," Albert said.

Then I shouted at the top of my voice. "Get that bloody door open."

As soon as I'd done it, I wished I hadn't. They all nearly jumped out of their skins. Charlie was so shocked he stumbled and fell over one of the chairs and on to one of the bench seats. Then he started gasping for breath. I thought, *Oh hell, don't tell me he's going to croak it.*

We laid him down, and after a couple of on the house whiskies, he came round. I was bloody scared. I got some of the younger lads from the games room to put the tables and chairs back.

Then Albert said, "You know, Barry, you couldn't have barred me. I am the ex-president of this club. Twenty years as president and thirty-nine years in all serving on this committee. You can't bar me, lad, no way."

I humoured him. I said, "No, you're right, I couldn't bar you, Albert", even though I knew I could.

Then both Charlie and Albert, followed by a few of their cronies, swaggered off to the bar like a gang of Del Boys.

Now I just have to sort the women, I thought.

BEV

Right performance today. Woke up, got ready and went to open the bedroom curtains.

There's cows walking about the street, looked like hundreds of them. I heard later that the cows had escaped from Jones' farm. They said it was about thirty but it looked like a hell of a lot more to me. They were running (well, walking mainly, cows don't seem to run much) all over the village. It was chaotic. They were going into the shops, into gardens, grazing on folks' lawns.

Connie next door was frightened to death. She told me later that she'd heard this noise at the door, opened it and came face to face with this big black and white cow. It mooed right in her face, its breath steaming up her glasses. She let out a scream and slammed the door in its face. It wasn't a happy cow, and it wasn't a happy Connie. She had to watch through the window while it trampled on her lawn and ate her rhododendrons.

I went round and sat with her for a bit, and we ended up laughing. I told her Barry will straighten the garden up for her.

Apparently one got into the library, and once it was in, it couldn't find its way out. It did a right big cowpat on the library floor, then walked it all over the library. It was knocking into the bookshelves, into the desks. It was eating the plants and mooing at the top of its voice. Right commotion.

The young lads were taunting them on the street, showing off in front of the young lasses. They'd run up to the cows and right into their faces, shout, "Boohoo, cow." It was very dangerous, I thought. One lad tried to mount one but it was too high for him, you don't realise how big and tall cows are.

I had to go to work and they were everywhere. I took Barry's big fishing umbrella with the spike on the end, in case one came too near to me. I had to divert every time I saw a cow, I wasn't walking past one of them. It took me ages to get to work. I was dodging in and out of shop doorways, sneaking around corners. It was like I was in some gangster movie.

They came into the garage forecourt. They were eating all the flowers on display outside.

All the traffic was held up. The police came. Farmer Jones and his workers were running all over trying to round them up. It seemed to take forever. They must have been on the loose for about six hours. It was a right performance.

The damage they did, though, you wouldn't believe. I hope Farmer Jones was well insured.

The men have asked the ladies' section committee to go into the office for a meeting. That's me, Cheryl, Geraldine and Rose.

Let's see what is on offer. Full membership is what we want.

Rose can't go. She's got a date with Alan again, the man with the thirty-nine hanging baskets and mucky fingernails. She says if she can't have Wayne, the love of her life, then anybody will do. She sounds a bit desperate to me.

BARRY

There were cows all over the village today. They came poking their noses into the club. Dennis was on the door and he came running in; he was frightened to death of them. I had to go and shoo the blooming things away. They are nosy beggars.

It caused a bit of excitement for the oldies. They were telling cow jokes. I think their jokes were aimed at the women though, not at the animals.

The committee have offered the women the Men Only room on a Saturday night and they practically laughed in our faces. I knew they would, it's a matter of pride with them now. They said they'd got this far; there was no turning back. Bloody Albert and Charlie and their little gang – it would have all been settled if it hadn't been for their stubbornness.

BEV

Went to The Bell tonight. The lasses were in.

I asked Rose how her date went with Thirty-Nine Hanging Baskets.

"Okay," she said. "If I avert my eyes from his fingernails, he's quite nice. He said it's his birthday next week and he wants to take me somewhere nice. So I thought I would buy him some gardening gloves as a pressie."

We didn't leave till well gone eleven. I walked home with Geraldine. When we got near to their house, we heard this singing. Then when we got to their house, we just gazed at each other, gobsmacked.

There was Baz, worse for wear on their front lawn, looking up at the bedroom window singing, at the top of his voice, *You Are My Heart's Delight*. He must have thought that Geraldine was in bed.

We stayed out of sight and watched him. We couldn't stop laughing.

There he is shouting, "I love you, Geraldine. I love yer." Then he shouts, "If you don't come to the window I'm going to take all my clothes off and lay down and die of pneu...pneu...pneu...Flu." I think he meant to say 'pneumonia' but his mouth wouldn't say it.

Then he started undressing, first his jacket, then his shirt, then his trousers. He's now singing *Davy Crockett*, king of the wild frontier, dressed only in his yellow Y-fronts and string vest.

I looked at Geraldine; I thought she would stop him there, but she didn't. Then his string vest came off, then his yellow Y-fronts, which he slung into next door's garden.

"He'll not get them back," Geraldine said, an angry look on her face. "You can bet your life they'll be on their washing line next week, Frank will be wearing them. They've got our garden rake – Frank borrowed it last winter to rake up the leaves. He now swears blind it's theirs." I thought she seemed less happy about the neighbours than she did about Baz stripped naked, singing.

So there is Baz, totally naked except for his socks. Then he lies down on the lawn, showing off all his manhood, shouting at the top of his voice.

"You are my heart's desire, and can we have a shag, Geraldine?"

I could not stop laughing. Then the neighbours' lights started to come on and folks were opening their windows.

Geraldine rushed over and kicked him right where it would really hurt. "Get up, you dozy drunken beggar," she said.

He looked at her, startled, then he said pleadingly, "Can we have a shag or what, Geraldine, love? I am desperate."

She gave him a push and said, "Get in, you fool. You've lost another pair of Y-fronts now."

He said, "Is that a yes?" I was laughing my head off.

She made him pick up his clothes. Then she placed her handbag in front of his doodah and pushed him into the house.

All the time he was saying, "Let me have a shag, Geraldine. Please, love, I'm desperate, I am, I'm desperate."

Geraldine gave him another big shove and said, "Get in."

As I was leaving the two of them, he throws his fist in the air and shouts for all the neighbours to hear, "I think that was a yes."

I walked home laughing. But there was part of me that was jealous of Geraldine: two men want her, and I can't get my own husband to want me. Me and Barry need a long talk, although I get the feeling that it might be too late for that.

I know I'm fat and I'm no Jennifer Aniston. But I've got to have an answer from him. I'm not going to live like this. I'm going to get out, divorce if things don't change.

Hopefully I've got a lot of years in front of me. I need somebody who needs me. Somebody who is prepared to strip off naked and serenade me in the front garden if needs be.

BARRY

Went for a walk down to the woods today, and I am ashamed to say I stood for a few minutes and watched a young couple having sex. What is up with me?

Then I went to the tree again where me and Bev used to go, and I looked for the carving that I did all those years ago.

Barry loves Bev.

I stood a while, thinking. This trouble at the club seems to have left everybody at loggerheads. The village was never like this. It now seems to be split into groups. If I had my way I would let the women have full membership and if they want to be on the committee, so be it. We would cope with that when it happened. But my hands are tied.

When I got back home I noticed Connie's door was open. I went in and she looked awful, real pale and she had a gash on her head. She said she had fallen. I know she is on warfarin, which can make you bleed internally, so I thought the best thing was to ring the hospital. The paramedics were there within fifteen minutes. They gave her a going-over and decide she needed to go to hospital just to be sure. I went with her and they are keeping her in overnight to keep an eye on her.

BEV

Went to the hospital to visit Connie. They have given her a brain scan to see if there is any bleeding, and it was clear. They're keeping her another night. I said I would fetch her tomorrow morning. Bless her, she is so frail. When I got back home I went into Connie's and cleaned the place up for her. She should be in a home really.

The lasses came round for a cuppa. Cheryl said she wished she hadn't said some of the things she said on the television interview. Ralph wasn't too pleased with her. They'd had a bust-up.

"No, it was good. You were only telling the truth," I said.

"It's not just about the club," she said. "All that I'm feeling about his relationship with his ex-wife came out. It was quite ugly."

We were all gobsmacked when she told us she'd packed her bags and gone to her mother's. She feels she plays second fiddle to his ex.

"His son is thirteen, in a couple of years he won't be wanting his dad. They're having sex at fifteen. He'll be spending all his time with the lasses," I said.

"Yes, that's what Ralph said. It's not his lad, it's her, his ex. I hate her."

Then she surprised us all. She told us that Ralph had followed her to her mother's, they had had a long talk, and he'd asked her to marry him.

We all wanted to know what her answer was. She had said yes. We all whooped.

"Hey, but you said you were going to have the reception at the club when you got married," Geraldine said.

"We are." She nodded.

"Have you thought this through?" I asked. "In the church, all the committee men on one side, and all us women on the other side, looking daggers at each other."

We started laughing.

"Then at the reception all the pent-up anger would come out," Rose said.

I chirped up, "Aye, Geraldine would throw trifle in Baz's face. Rose would floor Dennis and Slimy Sam, and I'd bash Barry with the top tier of the wedding cake."

"Yeah, just like a normal wedding," Cheryl said.

We howled laughing.

Cheryl said it wouldn't be this year, so hopefully this problem will be solved by then. We all said we blooming hope so.

So we have a wedding to save for and look forward to. I hope to God she doesn't let Father Randy Peter Pickles marry them.

Oh, I want a dog. I've been to see these little puppies at Mrs Gordon's. They're so gorgeous, but they're not ready to leave their mother yet. Jackapoos, cross between a Jack Russell and a Poodle. I don't know whether to put a deposit on one. There's a little brown one with white ears, so cute.

I told our Julie, and she said, "What do you want a dog for, Mother? It'll piss and poo all over the place. It'll be mi dad who ends up looking after it while you're at work. I think you'd better ask him first."

I'd really like one, they are so cuddly. If you haven't got a man to cuddle, get a dog. That's what I say.

BARRY

I've got myself in right bloody trouble today. I have smacked
that reporter from the *Star* newspaper. He just goaded me
with stupid accusations about us lot being male chauvinists.
I don't know what I was thinking of.

I kept telling him to leave the property but he
wouldn't budge, just physically pushed at me till I lost
it; I lashed out at him and hit him right in the face. He
stumbled and nearly fell in front of a brewery wagon that
was reversing into the car park. Thank God he didn't or
I would have been done for murder. I had to grab him
out of the way; he was dead shook up. I felt really sorry
for him.

I shouldn't have let him provoke me like that. I should
have walked away, gone into the club. He couldn't have
followed me in there. What a bloody mess. Things are just
spiralling out of control.

Next thing two police cars came screeching into the
car park, lights flashing, and four big coppers jumped out.
You'd have thought there'd been a murder. They arrested
me, handcuffs, the works. They bungled me into the car.
Bent my head like they do, so I didn't bang my head on the
door frame. I bet they used to get sued for that. Folks sue
for anything these days.

Everybody came out of the club, jeering.

"Haven't you got any real crooks to catch?"

"He's innocent."

"The reporter hit him first."

The coppers ignored all the comments. They were concentrating on arresting me.

I spent the night in jail. I had to make a statement. I told them about how he's been harassing the club members. They weren't interested. The only thing they wanted to know was did I hit him? Well, I did.

When I was a kid we had one copper in this village. He would ride around on his bike. Everybody knew him. Disney was his name, and he would often clip us kids around the earhole for doing something we shouldn't have. But this lot today…

BEV

Got up early and fetched Connie from the hospital, she seems fine now. I'd done some stew and I gave her a dishful; she will just have to microwave it later. I'll nip in tonight after work, make sure she settled alright.

What a shock! When I got to work, the boss starts asking me about Barry being arrested. It was all over the village and I knew nothing about it, I felt dead daft. I didn't know Barry hadn't been home all night. So much for having separate bedrooms! He obviously didn't want to use his one phone call to ring me. He must have been released after I left for work.

He'd been asking for it, that particular reporter, drove us crackers with his questions. If Barry hadn't hit him, somebody would have eventually.

Clive had to bar all of the reporters from The Bell, but they still waited outside to see if they could get some juicy bits of gossip. They've been a nuisance. Following us about, hanging around the village to see if they can talk anybody into giving them news of where and what we are at. They've even found out where Cheryl lives and there was one outside when she went to work one day last week. He offered her ten quid to spill the beans. She told him where to stuff it. We are getting to realise what it's like to be royalty.

Everybody's on Barry side, we've all closed ranks. Folks are coming out in their dozens to say they saw the reporter hit Barry first. If it goes to court they all want to be witnesses. One silly sod wanted to give Barry a black eye as proof. Bit late now; the coppers have already seen he hasn't got one.

I didn't mention it to him when I got in from work. He was very quiet, thoughtful. He usually likes to watch the news, but he didn't, he just sat, stone-faced, in his armchair. We will just have to wait and see what comes of it now.

I always knew Dennis and Slimy Sam were crackers. The drunken pair had put women's tights over their faces with the gusset around their necks and one leg dangling down the back. Then they waited near the bins round the back of The Bell, and when Clive went out back Dennis grabbed hold of him while Sam pushed what Clive thought must have been half a cucumber in a sock into his stomach. Sam told him to stop the women going into The Bell or else he'd regret it.

Clive said he couldn't stop laughing – not only did he recognise their voices but the silly sods had their committee badges showing. He said their breath stunk of booze; he could smell it even through their tights. He said they got right mad when he wouldn't stop laughing. They run away swearing, he said. He came back into The Bell laughing his socks off.

When he told us we were in uproar. But what it shows is that the men are getting desperate or drunk, or both, more like. And men like them are running the club – no wonder it's going down the nick.

I'm beginning to think it would be good for us all to have women on the committee.

Rose's date with Thirty-Nine Hanging Baskets went well. She says he took her to a fab restaurant, and she gave him the gloves for his birthday. He was right chuffed, she said. And they had a good snog.

Cheryl asked, "Are his fingernails any cleaner?"

"A bit, I would say," she said.

Geraldine said, "Rose, you are seeing what you want to see because I think you are in love. I bet his fingernails are just as mucky as when you first met him."

Rose didn't answer that one.

I had the feeling Geraldine was probably right. I think Rose should tell him to get them scrubbed.

BARRY

I'm being charged with assault.

They took my photograph and DNA, can you believe?

They know what I've done. Hit a man in the face – surely that doesn't warrant them taking my DNA? And they can keep it on file as well, I bet.

They'll probably try and prove I'm some serial killer now they've got my DNA. I'm really pissed off about that, bloody coppers.

First thing I need to do is get a good solicitor. Ralph has recommended one. He used him when he bashed a fella that was sleeping with his first missus. He got him off on a technicality.

It's all getting too much for a man; roll on next year.

Now she's on about getting a puppy. What do we want a blooming puppy for? It'll be me looking after it, clearing up its shit and pee and taking it for walks. I don't need anything else to worry about; I've got enough on my plate for now, thank you. Bloody puppies.

Baz came into the club, his face as long as the High Street. Says he's pissed off. Geraldine's doing nothing for him. He says there's no sex. He has to get his own dinner, wash and iron his own togs. His shirt didn't look as though it had ever seen an iron.

It's much the same story as most of the blokes are telling.

I do my own stuff anyway. When is it all going to end?

BEV

I can't believe it: Barry is being charged with assault, and they've took his DNA. What a liberty.

He had it coming, that reporter. Hope he trips and falls flat on his face and a dog poos on him.

I have been eating like a pig today; it's because of what has happened to Barry with the police and that. Whenever I'm feeling a bit down, what do I do? I turn to food.

One of the lasses at line dancing told me she takes a double dose of laxatives every night. She's dead slim and she has chips and pie after the line dancing every week. I've been to the chemist to get some and I'm starting tonight. She says if I take them early evening they should work in the morning, which would be great for me seeing as I don't have to be at work till two.

I couldn't find my keys again; they were in my shoe. I'm going to have to have them on a chain around my neck.

Geraldine came round for a cuppa and a pikelet. She's on a high. She never stops talking about the Reverend Peter Pickles. She's getting on my nerves now.

She tells me she thinks he must have had affairs before, because the nipple clamps didn't look quite new; some of the paint was peeling off.

I had to laugh. I was hoping she wasn't going to say the G-strings were second-hand as well.

And she says they now have this little sign when he's giving a sermon. If he scratches his nose that means he's got an erection under his cassock.

I nearly choked on mi buttered pikelet at that revelation. Erections during the service, I've never heard anything like it.

"What if he was having an affair when he married our Julie and Dan?" I asked her.

"Did he scratch his nose?" Geraldine asked me.

"I can't remember if he scratched his blooming nose or not, it was five years ago. I hope they're legal, she's got two kids." I was getting worried.

We decided it was legal. What goes on under a cassock can't possibly negate a marriage.

Then she tells me Pickles asks her to go into the church after they've…well, whatever they get up to, and she has to confess to him in detail for her sins, for doing it with him in other words.

Now I'm thinking. What does Pickles get out of that? He must get something out of it. I bet he fiddles around with himself in the confessional booth while she's describing their sexual activities. So who does he confesses to then, the bishop? I very much doubt it. I've read about these kinky priests. Geraldine ought to stay clear, but I bet she doesn't. She is besotted with him.

BARRY

My squirrel is dead. I took him some apple and he wasn't there. Then I saw him. He looked like a dog had had hold of him, or a fox perhaps.

I was really upset, poor little thing. I picked him up and tears filled my eyes, daft beggar that I am. I found a branch and I pulled away at the earth until I'd made a little hole. I placed him in my handkerchief, wrapped him up and I laid him in the hole, then I covered it with earth. I said a few words. Well, that's a sad end for my little pal. I will miss him.

We had a beer delivery today. I was surprised that even without the women's custom we had sold a bit more beer than usual. So the concerts are working, but think what we'd sell if the women were here.

I've been for a job interview, delivering motor spares. I got on right well with the manager, nice bloke. He plays *Call of Duty* on his computer so we had something in common, and he gave me some hints.

I think I might stand a chance with this one. Fingers crossed.

Spent a few hours cleaning up Connie's garden, they've made a right mess, them cows. The rhododendron bush has had it; bloody cows had trampled it. Lovely colour, it was, a nice light blue. Connie was right disappointed, so I went to the garden centre and got her another one. Poor woman – if it weren't for me and Bev I don't know what she'd do; Bev is ever so good to her. She's got two sons, one lives in Southampton and the other is in the Middle East. So she's nobody. But I'm glad to say that Bev always makes sure she's okay and that she's got what she needs.

She's very good like that, Bev. Connie wanted to pay me, bless her. She knows I'm out of work, but I wouldn't take anything. How can you take money off an eighty-eight-year-old? Later she came round with two cans of lager for me. She is a lovely old lady. I accepted gracefully, I knew she wanted me to have them, bless her.

BEV

Oh my God. I think all my insides came out down the loo this morning. I'm in a right state. Instead of taking two senna tablets, I took three. I daren't go out in case I have an accident. I've had to ring the boss and tell her I'm not well. I didn't tell her it was self-induced. I'll just have to watch the bedroom telly, it's the nearest to the loo. And I am missing my chocolate. Awwww! No, I am not just missing my chocolate, I am *ultra* missing it. It's like I'm having withdrawal symptoms. Well, they reckon chocolate is addictive.

I was counting up the amount of chocolate I must have been eating in a week. I could have opened a shop with it. I am going to have to be very firm with myself.

I'll be walking past a shop, and I'll be arguing with myself whether to go in or not. And the me that says, *Go in* always wins. I'll go in and buy loads of things. I can't stop myself. I know what I'm doing is wrong, but I still have to do it.

I suppose it's like a gambler; they have to go in the betting shop. Or an alcoholic; they have to go to the pub.

Chocolate – not one bar; three or maybe even four. Cakes, biscuits. I can't just buy a bit, I have to buy a basketful. Then I come home eat till I feel sick.

Then the guilt and anger come over me. So I take the wrappers off the uneaten stuff and throw them in the kitchen bin. I push them right down to mix them up with all the other household rubbish. The reason: so I won't try to get them out later. I have to unwrap them or I'll just scrabble in the bin later and eat it. That's how addicted I am.

You see actors on telly when they are playing an alcoholic; they buy a bottle of booze, start to drink it, then change their mind and pour it down the sink. Well that's me, only with sweet stuff and the waste bin, not the sink.

The doctors go on about people being addicted to drugs, booze, gambling. But it seems to be no big deal if you are addicted to chocolate, cakes, sweets and the like, and it is an addiction, it is.

It's an addiction I've got to fight.

I have decided to sell my big vibrating machine. Let somebody else get shaken brain syndrome. I bet I only get half what I paid for it. I'll put it on Facebook.

Rose rang; she is in love with Thirty-Nine Hanging Baskets. She said she bought him a nail brush and he's took the hint and his fingernails are dead clean, so they had a long bonk. I am happy for her, but I just hope she isn't rushing into this.

"Did he like your heart-shaped pubics?" I said.

"When he knew I'd had them shaped especially for him he was delighted." She giggled.

BARRY

I've been to see the solicitor. He said it's easier and cheaper to plead guilty. Worst-case scenario is a few months in prison. Best a fine and community service. Why did I let myself be drawn by that bastard reporter?

So one of the effects of the trouble at the club, which I have tried my hardest to solve, is that I might go down. Bloody brilliant!

And on top of that, they rang about the spares delivery job – sorry, but someone else suited them better.

Oh well, if I go down I won't need a job. And the way my luck is running, I will most likely go down. Life at this moment in time is shit.

BEV

I was in a cubicle of the toilets in The Bell and I could hear some of the women talking, so I quietly waited and listened.

I don't think they knew I was there, or perhaps they did!

The conversation wasn't very complimentary about the ladies' section committee, in other words, me, Cheryl, Rose and Geraldine.

They said in no uncertain terms that they are getting fed up of boycotting the club and coming in The Bell. They said it's costing them more. The Friday night free chips that were lovely at first are now cold and last Friday there were none at all. The crisps and nuts have disappeared off the bar. The toilet paper isn't replenished regularly. You always have to have tissues in your bag just in case, before you dare go for a pee.

They were also very scathing about Cheryl getting her face on the telly in her Marks and Spencer's clobber, as they called it.

"Who the bloody hell does she think she is? Photos in the paper, radio interviews, Mrs Posh Celebrity," they said.

I waited until they had left the loos before I came out. I told the others.

Cheryl was a bit put out about it. She said, "If shopping at Marks' makes me posh, then posh I will stay."

They'd all heard similar mutterings. The women's resolve was crumbling. The men must have heard the same gossip. That must be why there's no movement towards full membership for the women. The men know that the women's resolve is starting to crumble, so they are playing the waiting game.

If we have to go back some of the men will never let us forget it. Charlie and Albert's lot especially.

"And Baz," said Geraldine. "He'll not let it drop."

"We are going to have to think carefully about this," Cheryl said.

When I next went to the bar, I said to Clive, "Are we having chips on Friday?"

"If I can get hold of some spuds, love," he said, shaking his head as though I was asking him to get some heroin.

I haven't noticed any shortage of spuds, I thought.

Rose and Thirty-Nine Hanging Baskets are still bonking. She said every one of his baskets has a name and he says he remembers them all.

"Does he remember yours?" Geraldine asked her.

"Not always. He sometimes calls me Diane," she said quietly.

We all said, "Oh."

But they are in love, she says.

She stopped her direct debit to the dating agency and she is now in a fight with them. She signed up for six months and they want the full amount.

Geraldine told us she'd had a big bust-up with Peter Pickles. She said she was doing practically all the cleaning at the church.

It was "Will you do this, Geraldine? Will you do that?"

She felt like he was making her pay for his sexual favours and she wasn't having that. She said he can't half turn the language out when he's mad. He was 'effing this' and 'effing that'. She still goes to church, but they are not talking. She thinks he's got somebody else now, because she's noticed he scratches his nose a lot during the service and she thinks she can see some movement under his cassock.

"Good luck to whoever it is. But he needs to replace his nipple clamps," she said.

The lack of sex with the Reverend Peter Pickles has put Baz and her back in the same bed. And silly devil she is, she's taught Baz a few of the sexual moves that Peter Pickles taught her. He now wants to know where she got them from.

Rose said, "Tell him you've read *Twenty-Nine Shades of Grey*."

"I think it's *Thirty Shades of Grey*," Cheryl said.

"Or *Fifty Shades*," I chirped up confidently. I think I must be the only one who's read it. I bet I have less sex, but know more about it than any of the lasses, with all the novels I read. We all left the pub sober and miserable.

BARRY

I've heard about my court appearance. It's in the magistrates' court. Hope it's not some jumped-up bastard who hates the working class.

It's not going to go down well that I am out of work.

The solicitor has asked me to get some character references from people that know me: doctor, priest, dole officer? I will definitely ask Ralph for one, he's articulate. If I ask Sam, Baz or Dennis I'll probably get sent down for years. I have just got to wait now.

I heard rumblings that the women's resolve is on the wane. Must hang on and see.

I've been staying up till the early hours of the morning playing this computer game. It's so addictive. I just can't sleep with all that's going on. I can see the trouble parents have trying to get their kids to study. Good job I've got headphones; wouldn't want to wake Bev. Trouble is, I'm getting up later. Still, it takes my mind off the other things.

BEV

Cheryl has called a meeting of the ladies' section committee at her house.

She asked if any of us had any thoughts about the situation and we said no.

She said she had been thinking and asking around the women and it was true that their resolve was waning. Cheryl talks very official when she chairs a meeting. If we don't try to solve it without losing face, then we four will either have to stay at The Bell, which none of us wants, or go back to the club with our tails between our legs.

I think we expected more than that from Cheryl. She's been the ringleader from the start; she was the one whose idea it was to boycott the club. Now she is more or less saying we have to give in. Geraldine told her so, which didn't go down well with Cheryl. The look on her face said it all.

"Without all the women's support it is over," she stated. "There is nothing I can do about it."

"Brilliant," Geraldine said. "We've done all that mouthing about full membership and what have yer. We're going to look right bloody fools."

"We can make it look as though we're thinking about the good of the club, which we are," Cheryl said. "We can tell the men that because we don't want to see the club go under, we will accept their offer of the Men Only on a Saturday night."

"Yes, providing it's cleaned up," Geraldine said.

"We might have to offer to do that ourselves," Cheryl said.

"I'm not cleaning the blooming club," Geraldine snapped. Tempers seemed to be rising. We all felt a bit edgy.

"You clean the church," Cheryl snapped back. "Or is that because you get paid?"

"I don't get paid for cleaning the church," Geraldine snapped back.

"And there was I thinking all along you got paid in bonks."

"Oh, don't let us fall out," Rose said, raising her hands.

But Geraldine got up and slammed the door on her way out.

We sat quiet for a minute or so. Then Cheryl got up and started clearing the cups into the sink.

"Anyway, we can think about it for a few days and then have another meeting. See if any other ideas come up," she said, a bit calmer.

I left with Rose. Her and Thirty-Nine Hanging Baskets are still going strong. They are planning a weekend away. He's paid for her have a tattoo done too, a rose on her shoulder. She said he called it "A rose for a Rose."

I felt a bit down. So I went to the Co-op for a bag of Maltesers.

BARRY

We are going to have to give in and let the women have the full membership they have asked for; we have no choice. If we don't, the club will certainly go under. I'm going to have to work on the committee. I did it with the Men Only; now I'll have to do it for the full membership. There's no alternative. I know what I should do: pack the bloody lot in; let somebody else take it over.

I can't stop worrying about my looming court case. I hope they don't send me down. I wouldn't stand much of a chance getting a job if they did. Who'd employ a jailbird?

BEV

I had this really strange dream. I woke up and it was still in my head. I lay there struggling to remember it all.

Me and the lasses were on the flat part of the club roof, singing, dancing and drinking. We were having a right good time.

Then the men came out and wanted to spoil it.

"Get down," Barry kept shouting. "Get down, get down."

I started on him, gave him what for; I said everything I was thinking. I called him all sorts. I was really awful to him. It's funny how your dreams know what going on in your daily life. It's very strange. Then in my dream it started to rain and we all got soaked. It ended there. I must have woke up.

I went into The Bell after work; didn't fancy going home. The lasses were in there. I got a lemonade and a packet of pork scratchings – I wasn't hungry; I'd been nibbling at work all afternoon. Unusual for me but I didn't want any alcohol. I felt rotten; must have been bladdered last night, I can't remember getting home or getting to bed.

Everybody looked a bit glum.

Then Geraldine said, "You got sloshed last night."

131

"Don't I know it," I said. "I had a right head on me this morning. Didn't fancy going to work either, but I had to. I daren't have any more time off."

Then she said, "Do you remember what happened?"

"Not a lot, no. Why, what happened?"

"You mean to say you don't remember?"

"No, I don't remember. Go on, tell me, what happened? Have the men conceded and given us full membership?"

"Do you remember us climbing on the club roof and dancing and singing?" she said.

"Oh my God, how strange, I thought that was a dream."

Then Cheryl butted in. "Do you remember throwing that bottle and hitting Barry on the head?"

"I *what?*"

"You threw an empty beer bottle at Barry. It hit him with a right clonk. He collapsed on the floor."

"There was blood all over the place," Geraldine chirped up.

I suddenly felt sick.

"Ralph had to take him to the hospital. He had to have a brain scan and a load of stitches. You practically knocked him unconscious."

Oh my God, what have I done? I thought it had all been a dream. Even then, in my dream I didn't throw a bottle at him. Unless my subconscious mind couldn't accept the enormity of it all.

I sat for a minute; couldn't get my mind around what I had just been told.

"Is he alright? Where is he?" I was shaking.

"He's probably where he always is, in the club," Rose said.

"Ralph brought him back to ours. He cried, Bev. Your husband sobbed his heart out. He had me and Ralph crying with him. We have really messed up big time," Cheryl said.

Without another word, I left The Bell straight away and went to the club to find Barry. I got some right funny looks. Nobody had seen him.

What have I done? I came home and he wasn't there. I rang his mobile, he didn't answer. I went into his bedroom, and his bed hadn't been slept in.

Oh my God, where is he? I felt sick.

I stayed up drinking tea. I'd taken a bottle of wine out of the cupboard and then put it back. I was listening for his key in the lock, but it didn't happen. *What is he doing?* I asked myself. *Why is he putting me through this? He knows I'll worry.*

I finally went to bed about two. I couldn't sleep. I got up about seven o'clock, pacing. Don't know whether I was angry or upset. Bit of both, I think. I had two cups of coffee. I thought, *Right, don't panic. Nobody saw him yesterday, so let's start by ringing around; see if we can find him.* I waited till 9.30. I thought that was a reasonable time.

I picked the phone up and then I thought, *No, what am I doing? Let him stew, he's doing this deliberately to punish me. Let him come back in his own time.* I know he's alright; he spent half a night telling Cheryl and Ralph about our marriage. That made me mad, talking about us behind my back. Perhaps he might not come back at all. Who knows – might not be bad thing, at least there'd be no arguing. I've got plenty of mates; what do I need a man for? I don't.

I rang Rose; asked her if she wanted to go for a drink. We went into The Bell for an hour, and I got a lot of looks but nobody said anything. I wanted to talk about it but Rose kept bringing the conversation back to her own love life and Thirty-Nine Hanging Baskets. Why is it that when you need someone to open up to for something that is happening to you *now*, in the present, others shift the conversation back to their own problems, which you've discussed numerous times? I feel as if I've known Thirty-Nine Hanging Baskets for a lifetime. Perhaps she was uncomfortable with what happened. Perhaps she thought I was in the wrong and didn't want to discuss it, who knows?

I went back home and went to his bedroom; all his clothes were still there. I started searching through his stuff for any sign of another woman – there was nothing. Well, there wouldn't be, would there? He's not going to leave evidence lying about for me to find.

It went through my mind that perhaps he has secretly set up another home with some other woman. New clothes, new everything. Perhaps he's bonking her; that's why he's not bonking me.

I rang work to say I wasn't coming in again, I told her I'd got a bad stomach. I don't think she believed me. She'll have heard about the rumpus at the club. She said to come in when I can. I wouldn't be able to concentrate anyway.

So I just waited, watched a bit of telly, did a bit of comfort eating. Looked through the window. I kept picking up my mobile to ring him, then changing my mind. He probably expects me to chase him, but bollocks to that. I decide to make some stew.

Didn't sleep much again. I felt worse this morning. I decided for my own sanity I need to know where he is. I mean, not just because it's Barry; if it was a total stranger I would want to know they were safe.

If he has set up home with someone else so be it, I will have to accept it. I will take him for what I can get, though. I am not making it easy for him, not after all the years I have put into this marriage, no way. I'll make him suffer.

I rang our Julie; thought she might know something. I didn't say her dad was missing – that would have panicked her – so I just asked her general things about the kids and what have you. I know if her dad was there or if she knew where he was she would have said, and she would have given me a mouthful for throwing that bottle at him, which I suppose I deserve. One thing about Barry, he has never been violent towards me – he's lifted his hand but never hit me. I must admit, sometimes my bloody temper would make a saint violent.

I got my phone book and started ringing around, asking if anybody had seen him. His brother, his sisters, his cousin Johnny. No luck. Where the bloody hell is he?

Why has life turned out like this for us? I started weeping, then had a coffee, then another weep, then another coffee.

Cheryl came round. I told her Barry had been missing two days and she was shocked. She said she'd not rung me because she thought we'd be trying to sort things out between us. We sat in the kitchen speculating about what could have happened. Where could he be? I suddenly thought that perhaps he'd had some memory loss, because of the wound to his head. He might not know who he is and be wandering around some strange place.

She said she doubted it because when he was at their house his memory was fine.

Cheryl thought that being as he hadn't taken any of his things, it might be a good idea if I rang the hospitals. I burst into tears at that. So Cheryl rang them. Nothing.

Then we decided to ring the local police. They just said he's a grown man and until he's been missing a reasonable amount of time there's not a lot they can do. But they took his name and details.

"Oh my God," I said. "What if he's in hospital and they don't know who he is? He's just some John Doe laid out unconscious. You do hear of people in their forties having heart attacks and strokes. They're not just for the old."

One of Barry's old school friends died of a heart attack at forty-two – forty-two! Devastated his family, it did. Oh no, I've got that wrong; he choked to death on a piece of steak. His wife said it was sirloin as well. You don't expect to choke on sirloin steak, frying steak, yes, but not sirloin.

I'm starting to really worry now. My mind's all over the place. Heart attack, stroke, accident, another woman?

Cheryl told me if he had gone off with another woman he would at least have taken some of his things. "Anyway," she said, "if Barry had another woman there would have been some gossip, nothing ever happens here without somebody seeing."

I lay in bed, thinking about our marriage. It's amazing when you think you might have lost somebody, how you realise what they mean to you. I looked at the clock: it was 5am. I realised there was no sleep in me so I got up. I looked in the mirror. My hair was all over the place, I'd got tea stains down the front of my jim-jams and I look like I've got two black bin bags full of rubbish under my eyes. I must have only had about four hours' sleep since it happened.

I made a cup of tea, then went and got the photo albums. Gosh, we haven't half took some photos over the years. Most were holiday snaps: us in Benidorm, Greece, Italy, Majorca. I looked at the fridge; all the magnets were from the places we've been, there are stacks of them. We have been so happy in the past – what is our problem? We don't talk, we just shout at each other. He never listens to me. Do I listen to him? I don't know, perhaps I don't.

I decided to write him a letter – well, I can't talk to him; we always end up arguing. Hope to God he gets to read it.

Dear Barry,

You are putting me through hell at this moment, wondering where you are and if you are safe.

I am really sorry about throwing that bottle and injuring you. I was sloshed, but that is no excuse.

I don't know what is wrong with me, why I get so angry.

I've been looking at the holiday snaps and anyone can see how happy we used to be. Laughing together, arms around each other. Love was definitely there, in buckets. Where has it all gone?

I can't help but think that you don't love me anymore. I know I am not attractive like I used to be when I was young. I know I'm fat, I do try to diet, but…well, you know.

137

Is there someone else? I wouldn't blame you if there is because ours is not a happy home anymore.

When was the last time we made love? Ages ago. It's obvious you don't fancy me anymore.

I just get so depressed about my body. Sometimes I feel like cutting my wrists.

Perhaps we should get divorced, so we can both find happiness again with someone else.

Regards,
Beverly

Ralph called at the house. He said he was going to organise a search party from the club in case Barry was in any sort of trouble. He didn't actually say a heart attack or stroke, but I bet Cheryl and him had talked about it.

"Where does he go when he goes for his walks?" Ralph asked.

"Down to the woods, I'm not sure which part," I said. They're big woods.

"Try not to worry, love. I'm sure it will all end okay. We'll do our best to find him. Hopefully he's just playing silly buggers," Ralph said. "And Bev, if Barry had another woman we'd know, so get that out of your head."

I thought, *Yes, it's easy to say that but you don't know we have slept in separate beds for the last six months.* Or does he? Would Barry own up to that?

As Ralph left, Cheryl arrived.

"I've got to do something," I told her. "I can't just sit here."

"Well if you're up to it we can join the search party and scour the woods?"

I knew I'd feel better doing something.

Cheryl told me to put on some decent shoes. She knows I'm not very good at buying sensible shoes. I found some old trainers.

She said she'd be back in half an hour, and that I had to try and eat something. I had a quick shower and did my hair, and I felt better after that. I did a bit of toast but it seemed to stick in my throat. So I sat and waited for Cheryl, my thoughts going round and round in my head. *Where is he?*

I haven't been down the woods for years. I wonder if that tree is still there, the one Barry carved *Barry loves Bev* on to. We used to go down the woods a lot when we were young. Living with my mother and dad, it was the only bit of privacy we had. They were dead thin, them bedroom walls.

My mother and dad never thought to go out and leave us alone for a bit. I think both our girls were conceived underneath that tree. Better not tell our Julie; she'll think she's part acorn.

BARRY

I'm back; the house is empty. I'm feeling guilty. I bet she's been frantic. I had to get away, get myself together, sort things out in my head. I felt I was going barmy with all that's going on around me. Hopefully she'll have done some sorting out as well. My bloody head hurts; I've had a headache since Bev threw that bottle at me. We so need to talk, but it's not easy, not easy.

I've got my court case coming up, got to get myself sorted out for that. Life is kicking a lot of shit at us.

After my last entry our Julie came. I was surprised. *What is she doing here? It's not her day to visit*, I thought.

She laid into me. She had been trying to contact me. I'd had my phone off. I didn't want to talk to anybody; perhaps that was selfish but that's how I felt and that's what I'd done.

Then she told me, her mother's had a heart attack and she's in the hospital.

Heart attack! Bev! What a shock. I felt my legs go from under me. I had to sit down. I couldn't believe what I was hearing. My first thought was to get to her.

She was in intensive care. I entered the room and there she was, laid in bed, attached to all these machines. I couldn't stop the tears streaming down my face.

Our Julie put her hand on my shoulder and nodded at me. "It's alright, Dad," she said. "You cry."

I took hold of Bev's hand and kissed her gently on the cheek; she didn't respond. I was hurting like I've never hurt before. My Bev, my wife.

I looked at her and the fear inside me that she might leave me was overwhelming. *Please God, let her get better, please.*

Then a nurse came in and we were asked to go and see a Mr Patel. He was the specialist who was looking after Bev. The nurse led us to this room and asked if we would like something to drink; we both said a cup of tea would be nice. The nurse left and we sat down. Not a word passed between us; we were both deep in our thoughts.

We were startled as the door opened – it was the nurse with our drinks. She left and a few minutes later in came Mr Patel with the ward sister. He told us straight out that Bev had had a massive heart attack.

"Is she going to be alright?" I asked. That's what I wanted to know more than anything.

"We can't tell at this point," he said.

My heart sank. Those were not the words I wanted to hear.

He told us that she was in an induced coma, which is helping with her recovery and it's the norm for them to do that. So we were not to worry about that unnecessarily. He said they had put a stent in her heart and that seemed to be working as well as could be expected.

"That's good, then?" I said.

"Yes, but you have to prepare yourselves. Mrs Allsop may have incurred some brain damage."

Brain damage? I was gobsmacked.

"I thought she'd had a heart attack?" I said.

"Mr Allsop, your wife has had a massive heart attack and she was dead for some three minutes. That is when any brain damage would have occurred. When the heart stops no blood gets to the brain, and although her heart is functioning well now, brain damage is a possibility. The crucial time will be when we take Mrs Allsop out of the sedation. We will know then how much damage, if any, there is to her brain. You must also prepare yourselves for the fact that there is a chance that she might not wake at all."

Me and our Julie just looked at each other, tears streaming down our faces. *He doesn't mince his words, this man*, I thought.

"If she is going to wake, she will wake within about twenty-four hours after coming off the sedation. That is when we will be able to make an assessment." His bleeper went off and he made his apologies and left along with the ward sister.

Neither of us moved; we seemed to be stuck to the spot. Then a nurse came and took us back to intensive care. We stood either side of the bed and wept. The nurse told us that nothing's likely to happen before she is off the sedation.

I needed to go home and sort some things. I couldn't speak on the way there. Our Julie was chatting away, trying to see the positive side. I couldn't see any positive side.

When we got home our Julie wanted to know where I'd been. I told her it didn't matter. She laid into me then, she said it did matter when her mother was so distressed that she had a heart attack that could kill her, because I'd decided to disappear for days. She called me a selfish bastard. She's right, I am.

I'm due in court tomorrow. What the bloody hell am I going to do?

Emotionally I want to be with Bev every minute. But practically I know I have to go to court. If I don't go, they will certainly put me inside, and at a time when Bev needs me most.

Both me and our Julie decided I have to go to court. Julie will go to be with her mother.

Our Julie went home to see to the lads. I got washed

and changed, then went back to the hospital. I stayed till midnight, just sat there, looking at her. Then home.

When I got home I found Bev's letter. I read it. I couldn't believe it: she thinks I don't love her. I've never said I don't love her. I do love her. Divorce?! What is she talking about? I read the letter over and over again, tears streaming down my face.

Went to the hospital first thing, everything was the same.

Then I went straight to the court. Ralph and my solicitor were waiting for me. They asked about Bev. Nothing I could tell them that they didn't know.

They kept us waiting ages. I did say my wife was in hospital, but it didn't seem to make any difference.

I stood in the dock and I felt like a blooming murderer, and they treat you like one.

Thankfully the good character letters did seem to make a difference. The magistrates read them, and I could see they read them all. My solicitor told the magistrates about Bev.

The waiting while they deliberated seemed to go on forever.

To my relief I got fined £400, plus 250 hours' community service, and I have to pay £200 in compensation to the reporter. Bloody reporter. They said I could pay it weekly but I want to put it all behind me, so I paid it there and then.

I was so relieved. I wasn't going down. They said they had taken my wife's condition into consideration.

I went straight back to the hospital.

I've been at the hospital two days now; I've just kept nipping off home for a shower and to change. No change in Bev's condition.

I've been kissing her, stroking her face, holding her hands, all the things we should have been doing before this happened. I've been talking to her, telling her all sorts of daft stuff. I've brought some CDs in; music from when we were courting. I've played them to her. God, I love this woman so much.

They are taking her off the sedation at the weekend. Both me and our Julie are nervous. It's the not knowing that gets to you. Neither of us are sleeping.

I want her to live. I've never wanted anything more in my life. If I could swap places with her I would.

I decided to answer Bev's letter. Hope to God she will be here to read it.

My dearest wife Bev,

First thing I want to say is, I love you. I always have and I always will. There will never be anyone else for me. I didn't know you doubted it.

I'm as sad as you at the way things have been for us. We have had such a rough time. First your brother dying, then your mother. Then me losing my job. It's been enough to knock us both for six.

The awful thing is, we have allowed these things to come between us instead of bringing us together.

You eat when you are depressed. I'm reluctant to admit it but it has affected my manhood, my libido. I have always fancied you, gal, like mad. You have always been

*and always will be the sexiest woman I know or want
to know. No other woman can touch you as far as I'm
concerned. Sweetheart, at the moment if I took fifty Viagra
I still wouldn't be able to make physical love to you. What I
regret most is that I've let you go on thinking it's something
to do with you instead of talking to you and explaining
that's it's me, not you. I should have been trying to do
something about it. I've shied away from the truth, I've
been embarrassed by it. I am so sorry, sweetheart. We are
going to have to do some straight talking when I get you out
of that hospital.*

I love you forever.
Barry x

They are taking Bev off the sedation tomorrow. I've always
been an atheist, but since Bev's heart attack I've started
praying to God. I suppose you could say I'm hedging my
bets.

I started my community service today. Our Julie went
to the hospital to sit with her mother. I told her to ring me
straight away if there's any change. I'm racked with worry.

My first job was to paint the outside walls of the
community centre. It's pebble-dashed, and it's hard work
getting into them crevices.

It was the pensioners' dinner club day. I noticed Mable
and Gladys' scooters parked outside. Then they came out.
Both of them were in smart coats, which they'd bought out
of their bingo winnings. As they were getting on to their
scooters, I could hear them marvelling about the fish pie
they'd just had.

"Oh, it was beautiful, that fish pie. Did you think it was beautiful?"

"Oh yes, I did, I thought it was beautiful. The most beautiful fish pie I have ever had."

"And the most beautiful fish pie I have ever had. I weren't too keen on the potato topping though, mine had lumps in it."

"No, I weren't too keen on it either. Mine had massive lumps in it."

"I think I preferred the stew we had last week."

"So did I, so did I."

You have to laugh at them.

Then they saw me, asked about Bev. They said they had a card and some chocolates for her.

Folks have been so kind. I don't know what to do about all the chocolates she has had sent her. They don't like flowers in the hospitals anymore. Hygiene, I suppose.

Then Gladys said, "What are you doing, Barry?"

"My community service," I said.

"Oh, and I thought you were painting the walls." She burst out laughing and so did Mable. They find anything each other says hilarious, them two.

Then Mable said, "He was a very nice young man, that reporter you beat up. Oh yes, a very nice man."

"Oh yes, a very nice young man, a very, very nice young man."

Then they trotted off to their scooters repeating, "Oh yes, a very nice man, a very nice man." They were laughing their heads off.

They got to the gate and both of them tried to get through first. I heard a clang. Their scooters had banged into each other. They are a giddy old pair.

I am suffering but other people just carry on as normal; it's just the way of the world.

After I'd finished my paint job, I thought I had better make a bit of time to go and see Cheryl, find out exactly what happened. I wanted to know all about it.

It seems that Bev and Cheryl went down to the woods to look for me, thinking I could have had a heart attack or stroke. Then Bev saw a man and thought it was me, and she ran towards him. Cheryl said after she'd run about twenty yards she just collapsed. She went out. Luckily the man Bev thought was me was able to give her CPR, while Cheryl called 999. Apparently the ambulance couldn't get near so the paramedics had to stretcher her through the woods, right back to the road. Cheryl went with her to the hospital.

Why wasn't I there? I feel so bad. If I hadn't gone off in a temper she wouldn't have had a reason to go down the woods. She wouldn't have had a heart attack. It's all my bloody fault. If I lose her I don't know what I'll do.

Ralph came to the house, asked if I needed anything. I told him no, I was managing. We have got some good mates, me and Bev. They are always there for you. He's took over the running of the club. I don't want the secretary's job back and I told him so. I've had enough of it. Too much responsibility.

She has been off the sedation for twenty-four hours now. I have never left her side. Hardly took my eyes off her. The hospital let me sleep in a chair at the side of the bed.

Then, thank God, her eyes started to flicker. I jumped up, went to the bed and spoke her name. "Bev, Bev," I kept saying. Then her eyes flickered, then she opened them. Tears rolled down my face.

She was obviously disorientated. I thought, *Please, God, let there be no brain damage*. I spoke her name softly and looked into her eyes, hoping for recognition.

The doctors came and they told me to leave for a while. I went to the phone and phoned our Julie, and she cried down the phone. Then I phoned Cheryl and asked her to phone all the others.

When I was allowed back in they said everything seemed fine but there would be some tests to do.

She kept going in and out of sleep. I held her hand. Then she opened her eyes and she said my name; her voice sounded so beautiful. I smiled at her and she smiled back. *Thank you, God, thank you, God.*

"Is that the cut the bottle gave you?" she said. "I expected it to be much worse."

I had to laugh. *That's my girl*, I thought. I knew at that moment that she was going to be alright.

"I am alive, aren't I? It's not a dream?" she whispered.

"You sure are alive, sweetheart, and this is no dream."

She went on to ask me what had happened and I told her the whole story what Cheryl had told me. She seemed to take it more calmly than I thought, but then she's always been a strong woman. I can't wait to get her home now. Things will change.

BEV

Sounds like I've had a bit of a bad time. Well, not just me – Barry and our Julie too. Must have been awful for them, wondering whether I was going to live or die. Still, at least I'm insured.

I'll never forget Barry when I first opened my eyes. He gave me such a big smile, with all his face.

One thing I am looking forward to is getting on the weighing scales. Surely being in a coma for days must have lost me loads of weight. Perhaps I should go into a coma more often.

My mates have all been to see me, kept me up to date on all the gossip. Barry doesn't deal in gossip; he's never interested. He says he's got a surprise for me when I get home. I can't wait.

BARRY

She was in hospital about two weeks in all, then they said she could come home, but her recovery would take a long time.

All her pals were waiting at the gate with bunches of flowers.

I asked them in but they said no, I'd enough on getting her settled.

She's got cards, flowers and chocolates galore. She is going to have to rest up, and I will make sure she does. I got her settled on the settee and then I went to fetch the surprise I had bought for her. When she opened the box, her eyes lit up. A little Jackapoo; he shoved his nose out of the box and gave a little puppy yap. She adores him – she's called him Alfie, after her dad. He's a right lively little chappie. We've decide that when she is well enough we are going to go walking, and what better incentive than taking out the dog?

BEV

Gosh, it's good to be home. Barry's been great.

Apparently I died for four minutes. I can't remember seeing any white light – perhaps I wasn't dead long enough? And I didn't hover above the trees and see my body being given CPR. I'm glad about that because I don't like flying. I think I remember seeing a few flames though, and a bloke with horns, ha ha.

BARRY

Bev's been home a week now and she is doing great. Doctors have said she should make a reasonable recovery in time. Her young age will help that recovery.

Her heart is damaged; there is nothing they can do about that. It's up to us now. She can't go on living the lifestyle she has been living, and that is going to mean a lot of changes.

In a few weeks she will be going to see the rehabilitation nurse, and I will definitely be going with her. The nurse will guide us through the lifestyle changes. She has already been to see Bev and she's a very nice woman, I think they will get on great.

She is going to find it very hard but she has to do it. I will be with her every step of the way.

Bev has now got to take this weight loss thing seriously. Less food, more exercise.

The lasses have been great; they have visited her, made sure she doesn't get bored. I've heard them laughing away. I expect it's at the men's expense.

We are going to get through this.

I took her out today for the first time to the local shops. Hospital have lent us a wheelchair.

Everybody was stopping us, and she enjoyed the attention. She was joking with everybody. She was full of life, telling her story over and over again.

Things seem great between us at the moment, but I know eventually we will have to do some straight talking. Or perhaps we don't need to talk, perhaps the shock we've had has sorted things out for us. We both know where we went wrong. Well, I do. Hope she does. I'll play it by ear. Let's just enjoy what we have at the moment.

I am going to pack my job search in for a while till I think Bev is well enough to be left on her own. My redundancy money will see us through. Then I will start searching in earnest.

I've packed in the secretary's job at the club. Apparently Ralph has been doing a great job while I've been busy.

The Saturday concerts are doing well and the overspill – mainly women – are in the Men Only. Ralph got some of the younger men to give it a lick of paint. Baz managed to get some cheap emulsion. Pink. I've heard that Albert and Charlie have started frequenting The Bell on a Saturday night. I expect to get their custom Clive is allowing them to swear and fart to their hearts' content. There's talk he is going to install a spittoon, I bet that's another of Albert's fantasies.

BEV

How is it that I feel happier than I have for a long time? I've had a massive heart attack, and yet I am happy. I feel the future will be good. I think I've got my Barry back. And that ugly mole on the side of his chin? What mole?

I've had a massive heart attack
I've got to get myself on track
No cakes, sweets, burgers or chips
Nothing sweet to pass my lips
It's going to be the hardest thing
Walking past the Burger King
I've tried the grapefruit, cabbage too
With that, oh God, you just fart and poo
But with my hubby by my side
We will ditch all that's fried
We'll go for walks and swimming too

Do stuff that is long overdue
Life will be good, I feel it now
Barry and me have made that vow
So come on, life, give us a break
We know that we must give and take
We're going to put each other first
It's got to be for better or worse
To survive all this we have to fight
For our life, for our love, for we know it's right